Watch Out for the Big Girls

J.M. Benjamin

www.urbanbooks.net

Urban Books, LLC
300 Farmingdale Road, NY-Route 109
Farmingdale, NY 11735

Watch Out for the Big Girls

ISBN 13: 978-1-62286-487-4
ISBN 10: 1-62286-487-5

First Mass Market Printing May 2017
First Trade Paperback Printing August 2016
Printed in the United States of America

10 9 8 7 6 5 4 3 2 1

This is a work of fiction. Any references or similarities to actual events, real people, living or dead, or to real locales are intended to give the novel a sense of reality. Any similarity in other names, characters, places, and incidents is entirely coincidental.

Distributed by Kensington Publishing Corp.
Submit Orders to:
Customer Service
400 Hahn Road
Westminster, MD 21157-4627
Phone: 1-800-733-3000
Fax: 1-800-659-2436

To all the strong and sexy women who come in all shapes, sizes and colors of beauty. This one's for you!

—J.M.

Prologue

2006

"Bubbles, wha'chu doin up in there?" The words of twenty-three-year-old Charles Chase, known to the streets as Chase, penetrated the closed bathroom door of his honeycomb hideout as he impatiently yelled out.

"I'm comin', baby," was the muffled response he got from the other side of the door.

"Well hurry up and bring that big ass out here then. Shit! You know I ain't got all damn day!" Chase cursed.

He reached over and picked up his chocolate-toned Gucci watch lying on the nightstand next to the bed. He let out a gust of hot air in frustration seeing that he was already fifteen minutes behind schedule. By now, he thought he would be receiving the best oral he'd ever had in his life, followed by the wettest and freakiest sex in existence, compliments of what he called his big girl jump-off piece, known in his neighborhood as Bubbles. Instead, he lay there with a full-blown erection that stood at attention. Chase stroked his hardness as he envisioned what he intended to do to Bubbles once she came out of the bathroom.

He had received a call from her about an hour ago informing him that she was just leaving the gym and was running a little bit behind schedule of their agreed time to meet up. Had it not been for the fact that he was horny, his fiancée was away in Atlanta, and Bubbles was the only one with the ability to make him cum quicker than any other female he'd ever been with, he would've canceled on her when she told him she would be late. Now here it was she was taking even longer freshening up after her workout session at the gym.

This fat-ass bitch, Chase thought in frustration. *She's been big all her mu'fuckin' life since I've known her and now she wanna start tryin'a lose that shit. Jack La-fuckin'-Lanne himself couldn't help her ass.*

Chase snatched up the half-smoked blunt on the nightstand and relit it. He took a long drag of the drug and closed his eyes to marinate in its euphoria to calm his nerves. In less than two hours, he would be picking up his fiancée, Deborah, from McCarran International, and he wanted to get his dick sucked properly before she returned. He felt like being freaky today, something he felt he couldn't be or do at home, but could do with Bubbles. Although he and Deborah had been together for five years and he loved her, sexually she just wasn't enough. He had known Bubbles before his street fame and fortune, since he was a kid, and had been addicted to the way her mouth felt on him and he felt inside her since then. On countless occasions he fantasized of Bubbles's mouth and wetness while Deborah performed oral on him and during sex. He wished Deborah could make him feel the way Bubbles did and then there wouldn't be any need for a Bubbles, he reasoned with himself, but that wasn't the case.

Chase took another pull of the weed then glanced at his watch for a second time. Another six minutes had gone by. "Bubbles!" he barked. The irritation was apparent in his tone. "Bring your big ass out here. Don't nobody give a fuck how big you are. I ain't fuckin' your rolls," he added, with a light chuckle behind his words.

The drug had taken effect. He was used to talking to her in that manner with no regard to how it made her feel, just as he knew Bubbles was used to hearing it. He had no way of knowing the impact of his words today though and how they had penetrated the other side of the bathroom door.

Twenty-two-year-old Tamara Washington, aka Bubbles, stared at herself in the full-sized mirror. The mascara and foundation she had just applied to her face began to run and smear from the tears that began to pour out of her eyes. She felt like a fool for crying over something and someone who couldn't care less about her, let alone have any type of love for her.

If only my girls could see me now. It was because of them she was actually there in the first place. She knew they'd be disappointed and upset if they knew she was in the bathroom falling to pieces.

They just don't understand, thought Tamara as she shook her head with self-pity.

What they had continuously coached her through was not any easy task. Especially when it involved the man she loved. For as long as she could remember, she had a schoolgirl crush on Charles Chase and carried a torch for him. Ever since he moved right next door to her in the Carey Arms Apartments when she had lived with her grandmother, he was all she ever wanted. It was love at first sight for Tamara. Chase was actually the first person to make her feel beautiful and wanted. When her grandmother would launch her verbal assault about her weight and eating habits, it was Chase who told her how pretty she was and how God had created her the way He wanted her to be. When other kids teased her in the neighborhood and in school, it was Chase who used to come to her aid and fight them off. And when all the kids used to play hide-go-get-it, it was Chase who she always wanted to catch her and it was only Chase she would let get it. He was her first and she gave it to him whenever and however he wanted it. He was the only one who had ever made her feel special. Once he started hustling, things became different; he became different. Girls slimmer and prettier became his primary targets and she became secondary, sometimes third or fourth.

Bubbles could recall as if it were yesterday the first time he had publicly humiliated her, making her feel lower than she never thought possible. She could never forget how excited she was to see him around their housing projects apartments one day after getting off the Cheyenne High School bus. To Bubbles, she remembered Chase looking like something straight out of *GQ* magazine, as he sat on the hood of his BMW 325i, while a pretty, chocolate-toned girl leaned between his legs and some of the project guys flocked around him. Until this day, she regretted ever speaking to him. Bubbles closed her eyes and relived the traumatic incident as the degrading sound of his voice filled her ears.

"*Chase, you know her?*" *Karmen asked in disgust. She shot Bubbles a twisted look and then looked up at Chase with a frown plastered on her face.*

"*What? Know her like what?*" *Chase looked from Bubbles back to Karmen.*

"*Man, you know you fuckin' Big Bubbles,*" *one of Chase's boys joked. The rest of his boys broke into laughter.*

Bubbles stood there with tears forming in her eyes. She was sure Chase would come to her rescue and save her the way he always had.

"*I know you ain't fuckin' with nothin' like that and tryin'a fuck with me too?*" *Karmen spat with attitude.*

"*Man, y'all buggin' the fuck out,*" *Chase barked.* "*I don't fuck with no fat bitches!*"

His words nearly caused Bubbles to faint. She felt as if she couldn't breathe and her heart nearly stopped. She became dizzy as the crowd doubled over in laughter. With what little strength she had left in her body, she took flight. Later that evening, Chase picked her up and apologized a thousand times as they drove through Winslow Park. Bubbles forgave him, like she always did, right before he pulled over and unzipped his jeans zipper in his BMW and guided her head between his legs.

That was the first incident, but it was not the last. Now here it was, after enduring years of mental, emotional, and verbal abuse, and settling for less, Tamara Washington came to the realization that Charles Chase was no different than the others who contributed to tearing her down and trying to break her spirits. She shook her head and laughed to herself, but there was no humor in her tone. It was more a self-pitying type of laughter. She couldn't help but reflect on the damaging words that had pierced her heart and broken her down like a double-barreled shotgun two weeks prior to today when she thought she was carrying Chase's child. The words *"You're not even worthy to have my baby,"* and *"All the dudes you fuckin', that shit can't be mine,"* echoed inside Bubbles's mind. She took one last look at herself in the mirror. She adjusted her bra and the straps of her negligee. "You can do this," she said aloud before she took a deep breath. Then she turned and reached for the bathroom door handle.

"Damn, what took you so long?" Chase complained as Bubbles entered the room. "And you still look the same," he added.

Bubbles flashed half a smile and made her way over to the bed.

"Yeah, come to daddy." Chase stroked his hardness.

Bubbles crawled onto the bed and grabbed hold of Chase's dick. She peered up at him, licked the tip of his helmet, and then wrapped her lips around it.

"Ooh yeah," Chase cooed. He looked down at Bubbles as she swirled her tongue around the head. The two of them locked eyes as she toyed with dick. A devilish grin appeared across Bubbles's face before she took all of him into her mouth. Chase's toes curled and his ass cheeks tensed up.

"Fuck," he moaned. Chase placed his right hand on top of Bubbles's head. "Yeah, right there." He pushed Bubbles's head down, tossed his head back, and closed his eyes while she devoured him with her mouth.

Bubbles took another glance up at him. She knew it was just a matter of mere minutes before her oral skills forced Chase to explode. She began to attack his shaft vigorously. She deep throated him like there was no tomorrow. This always had Chase squirming. He thrust his dick into Bubbles's mouth. She knew he always did that when he was about to cum. She tightened her lips and let him roughly sex her mouth. Five seconds later, Chase had reached the point of no return, and so did Bubbles.

"Sshiit, fuck!" He twisted and turned as if he were going into convulsions. "Agh! Fuck! Yo, what the fuck? Agh! Agh!" The sharp pain he felt to the side instantly changed Chase's pleasurable moans into painful cries.

But Bubbles paid them no mind. She was in a zone. She blocked his cries out as she stabbed Chase repeatedly in the midsection with the sharp blade she had tucked in her bra. The only thing on her mind was all the pain he had caused her over the years. Chase tried to fight off the attack at first, but because of the fact that he was high and never worked out a day in his life, his five foot five, 160-pound frame was no match for Bubbles's five foot nine, 195-pound frame that went to the gym five times a week.

Bubbles was so engrossed in the deadly assault that she hadn't realized Chase had long ago stopped moving. It wasn't until she felt a hand on her shoulder that she broke out of her trance. Bubbles looked up at Chase, who lay lifeless and wide-eyed on the bed. All the blood nearly caused her to vomit, but she shook it off.

"You did good, baby girl," the voice echoed in her ear.

Bubbles turned and looked back. She was glad to see her girls. They were standing there with admiration plastered across their faces.

"Normally, we would have had you handle this differently for business-related purposes, but he was no use to us. I made this one personal for you," the woman who she respected the most, known as Starr, announced.

A half smile appeared on Bubbles's face. The words brought comfort to her once nervous-wreck demeanor.

"Go clean up and get dressed."

Bubbles nodded and climbed off the bed. Ten minutes later, she exited the bathroom bloodless and clothed.

"You ready?" Starr asked, standing in the middle of the room.

Bubbles shook her head.

"Okay, place your right hand on your chest and listen carefully," Starr instructed. The serious look plastered across her face was enough for Bubbles to know this was no joke; that what she was about to commit to there was no turning back from. She took a deep breath and did as she was told.

"I am confident, I am bold, and I am beautiful. I am big both in heart and in flesh and I am who I am because God designed me this way. I am a woman who makes no excuses for who and what I am and I refuse to let anyone pass judgment. Most importantly, I refuse to be oppressed by any living man and will stop at nothing to ensure that neither myself nor my sisters will ever be. No man shall ever or any longer degrade me, belittle me, or disrespect me, nor shall they lay a hand on me in any form or fashion with or without my consent. I am a Double G, which means I am double the trouble and I am a Gangsta Girl. I swear that if another violates or crosses me or my family, the consequences and penalties shall be severe. Double G is not a gang; it is a way of life, a life I pledge to live until I breathe my last breath!"

Bubbles stood in awe and listened attentively until Starr had ended the Double G initiation pledge. As Starr recited the pledge, Bubbles could feel herself growing stronger with each word. She knew she had made the right choice.

"Do you accept this pledge?" Starr asked.

"Yes, I do." Bubbles nodded.

Starr grinned. "Good. Well then you're one of us now. Welcome to the family."

Bubbles embraced her as she threw her arms around her and delivered a warming hug. The two women standing in the background behind Starr nodded in agreement as they watched the exchange.

"Double Gs for life!" Starr chanted as soon as she released Bubbles.

As if on cue, her girls followed suit. "Double Gs for life," her two crime partners, Diamond and Felicia, sang in unison.

"Double Gs for life," Bubbles joined them, as she was welcomed into her new family.

Chapter One

Seven Years Later

As usual on a Saturday night, or any other night for that matter, the booming city of Las Vegas was lit up like the Hollywood billboard sign. Las Vegas Boulevard starting from Sahara down to Russell Road was in full throttle. The Sin City strip, filled with hotels and casinos such as the Aria, Planet Hollywood, Paris, Caesar's Palace, Bellagio, and Wynn, was infested with tourists from all over, and local Nevadans looking for action. Clubs like the Chateau, Pure, Drai's, and the Bank were some of the recommended spots to party, but the infamous strip was not the only place you could find something to get into when the sun went down. Not too far down and over, some of the elite money-getters from the East Coast, Midwest, and West Coast, along with some of the finest Nevada-bred women, pulled up in some of the most exclusive vehicles to the valet in front of another popular hot spot, while company limos escorted clubgoers to the front door of the establishment. The VIP entrance flowed while the general admission line to enter the frequented spot nearly wrapped around the side of the building.

Although Las Vegas Boulevard was one of the most popular streets filled with many nighttime attractions, on Highland Drive sat two main businesses that were guaranteed to be jampacked week in and week out and they nearly sat across the street from each other: the Treasures gentlemen's club and Club Panties.

Treasures was a plush two-story, exclusive strip club that claimed some of the most professional exotic dancers in the surrounding area. Despite Club Sapphire being the largest strip club in Vegas, Treasures stood out more. But, the difference between Treasures and the average strip club was that short-stacked customers couldn't last ten minutes. Your paper definitely had to be up and you had to be willing to spend it to get any attention in the hot spot. Everything was slightly overpriced, specifically for out-of-towners. There were hardly any regular drinks served in the club. The partygoers who attended on a regular basis turned it into a strictly bottle service affair, popping bottles of liquor starting at $750 and champagne starting at $1,500, with a two-bottle minimum per VIP section.

The dancers loved working there because no bills under tens were tossed into the air like confetti and if you did see dollar bills, countless bands were being popped in succession. Being that tens were the new ones, to make a statement most ballers tossed around twenties and fifties just to warm up. Needless to say, they got their money's worth. Even topnotch pimps paid to play, as they kicked back in VIP popping bottles while sending their flock of female solicitors in the crowd to work and recruit. Every dancer stepped her game up because it actually felt like a business, as opposed to a cheap thrill for loose change. Everybody claimed to be getting money, and to last a night in such a high-class environment, you paid to show it.

Most of the people who were still standing in line outside, anxious to get inside the club, complaining about the long line, began to quiet down as they heard a loud roar of thunder coming from far down the street. Many of them knew exactly what and who it was. Others just watched, waiting to see, while those who were illegally double-parked hurried to clear out of the four-lane street.

Out of nowhere, two matching chromed-out Yamaha R6 1100s came whizzing down the strip at top speed, with front wheels in the air. Each bike possessed passengers on the back, gripping the drivers for dear life, with protruding bottoms that required WIDE LOAD signs.

Seconds later, another four expensive-looking bikes came zooming down the strip directly behind the first two. They performed a series of stunts as the crowd they passed cheered them on. The men were extra hyped because the girls who were on the back had long hair flying from under their helmets, and fat asses revealing their thongs and ass cracks due to the low-rider jeans and booty shorts they wore.

All six of the machines met up down the street and made a 180-degree turn down by the entrance of the parking lot. They slowly rode their way back up in perfect formation. They were lined up side by side, blocking off the entire middle of the street, facing the way they had just come down. They paused in the middle of the street between Treasures and their destination, and waited. They fed their engines power blasts of gas each time they yanked on the throttle while the bikes were in neutral. The thunderous roar from the beginning had never ceased, or let up. It only grew louder. Everybody's attention was drawn to the booming bass that vibrated the concrete that came from the same direction the bikes had appeared.

All eyes focused on the two huge stretch Escalade XLs with limousine tints and monstrous chrome rims that came cruising down in slow motion, trailing each other back to back. They were accompanied by twenty more motorcycles of all sizes and models. The trucks stopped directly in the middle of the street, headlights to headlights with the first six bikes. Both sides of the trucks' back doors opened up simultaneously. The sound of Nicki Minaj's voice illuminated and blared out of the side doors' speakers of one of the SUVs, while Lil' Kim's voice illuminated from the other as two pair of beautiful, full-sized women stepped out of each Escalade and into the middle of the street. All eyes had definitely zoomed in on them.

The passengers on the backs of the first six bikes climbed off and removed their helmets, revealing their own beauty. The drivers of each R6 did the same. Some were surprised to see that who they believed to be muscular and husky men controlling the bikes were actually beautiful, full-figured females. Most weren't surprised. The Double G logo on the back of the half-cut leather jackets said it all.

The lines for both clubs were almost the full length of the block along the sidewalk. Across the street from Treasures was Club Panties. It was by far the largest upscale lesbian-only club ever known to exist. It filled the same capacity as any with just women. Most people from both clubs mixed and mingled on the sidewalk and in the streets. Club Panties was known for having a tougher crowd. The police frequented and had more incidents occur at the all-female establishment than Treasures ever since it had opened five years ago. On occasion, you could catch two bloody, wild-haired females with breasts dangling from torn blouses being escorted out of the club in handcuffs. With all that had transpired throughout the years, including a few altercations ending with someone losing their life, many could not believe the club still managed to remain open.

The drivers of the first six bikes pulled over and parked in front of Club Panties, while the two Escalades and the other twenty motorcycles created their own parking spaces in the vicinity as well. The back doors of one of the SUVs flew open and out stepped Starr, Diamond, Felicia, and Bubbles. The four sexy, voluptuous but deadly female passengers who climbed out of the truck led the way as they strutted toward

Club Panties. Necks nearly snapped as awaiting partygoers watched the four Amazon goddesses, accompanied by a slew of others like them, roll up stone-faced in their bike club's colors. They ignored the long line as everyone eyed them as they walked straight to the entrance.

The huge security guard acknowledged them and unhooked the velvet rope from the brass rail, while stepping to the side. Another guard in a full three-piece suit appeared from inside and escorted them through the dimly lit lobby. The four women strutted right around the walk-through metal detector. The next six strolled through the high-tech security machine stone-faced as the sensors beamed to maximum red, triggering the metal detector until the last girl cleared it. They were used to bypassing pat searches and entering the club with their weapons on them. Their leader made sure that was never a problem. After all, it was their organization that owned the club.

The only male security guard allowed on the premises, who worked the door, shook his head in disgust as he watched the logos on the back of the jackets disappear into the club. "Damn Gs," he uttered under his breath.

Most of the women who stood in line watched with admiration and envy while other onlookers stared with hatred and jealousy in their eyes as the head of the Double Gs led them and made their way inside the club. One woman in particular, Monica, who stood in line closest to the entrance, studied the crew as they received the royal treatment. She smiled to herself and chuckled under her breath lightly at the scenery. She shook her head while one of the female security guards checked her ID and shined the flashlight into her clutch.

"Care to share?" the female security guard asked.

Monica noticed the seductive look the female security guard had plastered across her face. She realized the female security guard had mistaken her own smile for a flirtatious one. She had almost forgotten that she stood in line of a gay club; and she was not gay. Let her tell it, she was bicurious. But she was not interested in the female security guard. She flashed another smile to match hers. Before she could conjure up something to say to let the female security guard down easy, a familiar voice came to her rescue.

"Nah, she straight. She with us," Felicia, one of the Double G members, announced. Out of her peripheral vision, Felicia had noticed the girl she had presented to Starr for consideration. She stopped in her tracks and backpedaled.

"Wassup?" Felicia nodded.

"Hey." Monica flashed the best smile she could conjure up. She sounded both surprised and glad to see her. The only thing that now stood between the two of them was the velvet rope.

"I got you," she told Monica then drew her attention to the female security guard. "I'm trying to figure out what you're waitin' for." Felicia looked from the female security guard down to the velvet rope then back at her.

The female security guard rolled her eyes and removed the velvet rope. She was moving a little bit too slow for Felicia's taste. She also noticed the partial rock stare she shot her way. She excused her tardiness, but her look did not go unnoticed. "Bitch, you better get yo' life." Felicia's body language spoke volumes.

Without meaning to, the female security guard rolled her eyes, which was followed by the sucking of her teeth. She knew exactly who Felicia was and knew she had made a mistake as soon as she reacted the way she had. Before she could clear the air, Bubbles was already by Felicia's side.

"Er'thing good, sis?" Bubbles looked from Felicia to Monica, then over at the female security guard and back to Felicia. Her hands rested on her massive hips. "And who is this?" She nodded her head in Monica's direction.

"That's what the fuck I'm trying to find out," Felicia chimed, never taking her eyes off of the female security guard. "And this is one of the newbies I been scoutin'," Felicia added, referring to Monica as one of their new, upcoming potential Double Gs.

Bubbles gave Monica a once-over. Monica just stood there stone-faced. Her eyes did a quick glance over by the entrance. The other Double Gs were making their way inside the club. Felicia's back was now to her and Bubbles. Just as she finished her survey of her surroundings, her and Bubbles's eyes met.

Bubbles flashed a half smile and broke the stare. She turned in Felicia's direction. Felicia's eyes were fixated on the female security. "Fee?" Bubbles called out. "What's up with this shit?" she wanted to know. She was ready to go inside and get her drink and party on with the rest of the crew, but had no intention of doing either until she was sure Felicia was good.

"This bitch gonna make me come out of character," Felicia looked over her shoulder and uttered to Bubbles.

Monica heard it also. Apparently, so did the female security. "Fee."

"Bitch, you know me?" Felicia cut her words short. She also caught the attention a few other Double Gs, who had now stopped in their tracks just shy of the club's entrance.

The female security guard's heart rate started to increase. A nervous feeling crept into her body. As tough as she believed herself to be, she knew she was outnumbered.

Monica watched the scenery as it unfolded. On the outside she may have appeared stoic but, on the inside, her nerves were all over the place and her mind was racing one hundred miles a minute. She wasn't sure if she had the stomach for it, knowing this was light compared to the stories she had been told about the Double Gs. Although men were their suggested targets, from what she knew of them, they didn't allow anyone to disrespect, cross, or refuse anything to them, just as she knew one word from Felicia and the female security guard's family could be pulling out the favorite black outfits for her funeral.

She wasn't sure if she could actually carry out what she had signed up for. There was no doubt in her mind she was nothing like the women in the organization she was trying to join. But it was bigger than her, she told herself for the umpteenth time. Monica grimaced as she continued to watch the altercation with Felicia and the female security guard. She felt for the woman. To her, it wasn't that serious. But if you were a Double G, like Felicia and Bubbles, it was very serious. She was well aware of the fact the Double Gs moved as one and would remove anything that got in their way. One wrong move from the female security guard and not only would Felicia be all over her like salt on fries, but so would Bubbles and the rest of the Double Gs looking on as well.

Although she held her composure, Monica wanted to cringe at the thought. She was all too familiar with how they got down. It was part of the reason why she was at the club tonight. She needed to know more than what she had read about or been told. All of that was circumstantial. She needed facts. And that's exactly what she intended to get.

People in line had already begun backing up out of the potential harm's way they were in, being too close to the arising altercation. Many of them also knew who Felicia was and knew she didn't play. None of the Double Gs did, but Felicia was mostly known for her violent demeanor. All onlookers' eyes shifted around from Monica, the female security guard, Bubbles, and Felicia, wondering and anticipating what would happen next.

Felicia let out a gust of hot air and shook her head. She was not in the mood tonight to be beating down or pistol whipping somebody like she normally would have for less. But there were too many people watching for her to let it go. She wouldn't be her if she did. "Is there a problem?" Felicia snapped.

Her sexy arched eyebrows formed as one due to the scowl that was now plastered across her face. She was already anticipating her next move based on the female security guard's response. All it took was one wrong word for Felicia to wipe the tough look off of her face. There was no doubt in her mind that she could beat the female security guard's ass. She had sized her up and concluded that, at five foot eight and 165 pounds, give or take, her body was no match for her solid, curvaceous one at six foot one and 220 pounds. She folded her arms.

In a matter of seconds, the female security guard's facial expression went from an ice grill to a submissive one. She saw a way out and she took it.

"No, Fee. I mean, no, not at all." The female security guard caught herself, remembering how Felicia reacted the last time she had said her name. She lowered her gaze. To say she was scared would be an understatement. Despite the cool summer breeze that filled the air, her black security tee began to soil with perspiration around the collar and up under her armpits. Beads of sweat began to appear on her forehead as if she was coming down with a fever of some sort.

"Oh okay, just making sure," Felicia stated sternly. She could see the fear written all over the woman's face. She was a firm believer in not forcing somebody into battle if they really didn't want a war. Had Starr been present, even if she had wanted to she couldn't have shown the female security guard any mercy. No matter coward or tough guy, if you violated or disrespected a Double G Starr demanded you be dealt with in the most degrading and sometimes unthinkable way. But Starr wasn't present and it was evident the female security guard didn't want any beef, so Felicia drew up.

"Just unhook this shit," Felicia commanded in an authoritative tone.

The female security guard did as she was told. This time she moved more like the hare rather than the tortoise.

Felicia winked at Monica as the female security guard unhooked the velvet rope. She then turned to Bubbles. "I'll catch you inside."

Bubbles nodded. She was convinced there was no imminent danger or real major problem. She spun around and made her way into the establishment.

"Anyway, why you didn't hit me?" Felicia asked as Monica put her ID back into her clutch.

She shrugged.

"You ain't gotta stand in line with them broke bum bitches. You fuck with us, and this our shit," she announced.

Monica smiled, but not at what Felicia had said. Her smile was credited to being one step closer to becoming a Double G, and one step closer to justice and revenge. She put on her game face as the two of them sashayed their way inside Club Panties.

Chapter Two

The Next Day

Aside from the soft moonlight that slipped through the black lace balcony curtains, the luxurious penthouse's master bedroom was fairly dark. The mood was perfect. India Arie's Pandora station had nearly repeated the songs in its rotation twice, but to Starr it felt as if it was still on the first song. She had lost all track of time. The state of ecstasy she was in had her in another realm and she had no intention of returning anytime soon.

For the past hour or so, her body felt as if it was being put through an intense workout that would never end. Her thick, shapely legs and inner thighs were well aware of the immense amount of time that was passing from the extreme pleasure. As her massive thighs cramped up on her continuously, she realized she couldn't hold them spread far apart and high into the air any longer.

Slowly she lowered the heels of her feet onto the shoulders of the woman whose head was buried between her legs. She clenched the satin bed sheets, bit down on her bottom lip, and closed her eyes as her love partner's lips smothered her clit and delivered flurries to it with her tongue. Starr tried to control her breathing. She exhaled lightly then inhaled deeply, but it was no use. Her heart raced faster and uncontrollably each time her partner's tongue made contact with her G-spot.

Diamond had a five-inch tongue that felt like pure silk, not to mention the fact that she was proficiently skillful. She paid perfect attention to Starr's rhythmic breathing patterns and involuntary body reactions. She adjusted her body weight and positioned herself between Starr's legs to support them over her shoulders. Diamond peered up at Starr and smiled at the passionate expression she bore on her face. She stiffened her tongue and slid it inside of Starr's wetness as she used her long middle and pointer fingers to part her outer walls. Hearing Starr moan turned Diamond on. She slipped her tongue out of Starr's love box and swirled it in a circular motion around her clit. Her face was close enough for Starr to feel her breath between her inner thighs. Diamond watched as Starr's sex grew wetter by the second as she blew warmth between her slit. She could feel Starr squirming underneath her as she took the underside of her soft tongue and rested it directly on the center of Starr's wetness. She applied firm pressure before she gently sucked on it. She kept her warm, moist mouth open just slightly enough for the open air to slip through the corners of her luscious lips and heighten the sensation.

Starr's body trembled. She gripped two handfuls of Diamond's long, curly jet-black hair like horse reins and held on for dear life. She could feel that she was drenched in her own love juices. She rotated her hips and thighs into Diamond's face. She rode Diamond's tongue as if it were a saddle. Starr quivered from yet another explosive orgasm as Diamond gripped her by the waist. She started shaking and going through convulsions, feeling like she was slipping into a soft coma. Her eyes rolled into the back of her head. It was as if she was destined for such a forbidden and condemned lifestyle. She savored the moment, but was abruptly interrupted by the sound of her cell phone ringing. Starr pulled the lower half of her body away from Diamond's face, and reached for the phone. The number came up as Blocked on the caller ID. She hated that but still accepted the call, aggravated by the disturbance and disruption.

"Whoever this is, call me back from an unblocked number," she said with attitude. She was just about to hang up, but the unidentified caller's words stopped her in her tracks.

"I wouldn't hang up if I were you," a male voice blurted out.

A puzzled look appeared across Starr's face. The caller immediately caught her attention. "Who the fuck is this?" She stared at the phone and then put it back to her ear.

"Don't matter," the male voice replied dryly.

She was in no mood to be playing games. She could already feel herself getting out of a sexual mood and transitioning into a more serious state. "Look, mutha—"

"You have an undercover agent planted in your organization. This piece of information is free. If you want to know anything further, it's going to cost you . . . a lot," the male voice cut Starr off.

A second later, the phone went dead in Starr's ear. She stared at the phone for a second time. She then looked down at Diamond with an untrusting eye. Still, she kept her cool, and kept what she had just heard to herself.

"Is everything okay, bae?" Diamond asked. She noticed the sudden change in Starr's demeanor.

"Yeah, everything's straight. I gotta go," Starr brushed her question off. She hopped up and began to dress. "I'll hit you up later," she informed her lover without bothering to turn and look at her. Her mind was too preoccupied by the words playing in her head from the anonymous caller.

"Damn! No kiss, no hug, no nothin'?" Diamond chimed.

Starr stopped and turned. She was already headed out the bedroom door. The phone call had her in deep thought. It was all she could think about. She didn't want to alarm Diamond.

"My bad, babe." She made her way back over to the bed and leaned into Diamond. She cupped Diamond's face and flashed her a loving smile. She gave her a deep, passionate kiss. Diamond tried to wrap her arms around Starr's neck and her long, muscular legs around her waist, only to be rejected. "I gotta go." Starr broke their lip lock and released Diamond's chin.

She stared into her eyes. She felt guilty for searching for betrayal in her lover's eyes. She didn't want to believe that she had just kissed her Judas. Starr shook the thought off. For all she knew, the phone call was bogus, even though her gut was telling her it was not a drill or a joke. She flashed Diamond one more smile. "I love you, girl."

"I love you too, Starrshma."

Starr let out a light chuckle and shook her head. Diamond was the only one she allowed to call her by her birth name without blacking out and getting pissed off. She was also the only one who made it sound like music to her ears, although she disliked her real name. *It can't be her,* Starr thought. *That's my rider right there,* she concluded.

"I'll see you later," Starr said and then she was gone.

Diamond hopped out of the bed and pulled back her room's curtains. She squinted from the sunlight that met her at the window. She hadn't realized how much time had passed since they had left the club and she and Starr had met at her house. She watched as Starr climbed into her green, black, and red Ducati. She forced a smile as Starr looked back and up at her in the window and blew her a kiss the way she always did. She hated the fact that she had just up and left in the midst of a heated and passionate moment, but she knew there was nothing she could do about it. She knew exactly who and what she was getting involved in when she first crossed the line and started dealing with her boss, but still she didn't like it.

There was no doubt in her mind that Starr would choose her work over her at the drop of a dime. That was a problem for her. She loved Starr so much that she would be willing to give it all up. She would risk any- and everything for her if it ever came down to it, she knew. She managed to return Starr's kiss. A few tears trickled down her face at the thought. As soon as Starr sped off, Diamond thrust herself onto her bed, buried her face in her pillow, and let out a loud cry.

Chapter Three

The college classroom–styled domain in the downtown Las Vegas federal building was filled with over two dozen law enforcement officials and representatives from every branch and department. The lead agents, head detectives, and top-ranking officers sat up front. Members from the Washington field office, the public corruption unit, and the organized crime division were called in by the director of the Federal Bureau of Investigation at the request of Head Special Agent Tom McCarthy.

The central air system pumped out an inconsiderable amount of low temperature that most of the law officials ignored with the help of the two-day-old coffee and stale donuts. For most of them, it was just like being back at the academy. They joked around and mingled among each other until the lights went out. The only sound that could be heard in the room was the film projector. The beam of a bright white light shot from the back of the room onto the white eighty-inch roll-down canvas screen.

Special Agent McCarthy stepped in front of it. His huge shadow reflected on the blank screen, making him appear much larger than his five foot seven, 180-pound pudgy frame as he stepped directly into the beam of light. All eyes were on him. Most hadn't met him personally, but he looked like he meant business. And he did. He made sure that every single person was paying attention before he began. His silent point was established. His patience remained untested.

Agent McCarthy wore a black tailor-made suit and black tie, with a white button-up shirt underneath. He adjusted his tie while clearing his throat. He stepped up in front of the cherry wood podium and cut the small brass overhead lamp on. It shined down on his notes. He quickly scanned through a few pages and then picked up a tiny remote that resembled a huge pen. He kept his thumb on the top button that controlled the projector. At the first click, a surveillance photo of a beautiful, young, full-figured African American woman exiting a nightclub appeared on the screen. It was hard to make out her estimated age range due to the way she was dressed in the photo. Agent McCarthy strolled over to the screen. He faced the audience as he spoke.

"This is Starrshma Fields, aka Starr. From what we know, she is the second-in-command of a powerful lesbian criminal organization. They call themselves the Double Gs."

Most of the officers and agents in the room chuckled under their breaths, but not without it going unnoticed by Agent McCarthy, who remained militantly serious as he continued.

"Now, I assure you that this is no laughing matter. This group of women is not to be taken lightly. That is exactly how they got so far, so fast. They are relentless; worst of all, they are perfectly structured. I also assure you all that in your entire career in law enforcement, you have never seen, or been up against, a group that warrants the continuing criminal enterprise statute such as this. I have personally been tracking this organization for the past nine years. We have reason to believe that this organization started out as a simple renegade lesbian motorcycle gang nearly twenty-three years ago. Since then, it has expanded into what it is today: an underground dictatorship dynasty." Agent McCarthy paused to take in the faces in the room before he continued. He could see that not many were following or took his words seriously.

"It was founded by an anonymous woman who they call Queen Fem," he continued anyway.

"Still to this day, we have no idea who or where she is. But we do know that Ms. Fields is the key to it all. She is the only one who knows how to get to Queen Fem."

A voice from the dark untimely interrupted, "With all due respect, sir, why is this our problem, or concern? From what we're hearing, they're just a group of Girl Scouts gone wild. Meanwhile, we've got real bad guys to catch, terrorists to fight, and dope dealers to bring down. How does a gay girl club warrant the devotion of every law enforcement agency there is?"

Agent McCarthy shook his head in frustration, knowing that the comments had probably come from some dumb local who thought ten years on the force gave him credibility as a decorated officer. Still, he upheld his professional yet stern composure as he continued.

"Without further interference, I'll tell you exactly how this warrants all our attention. This isn't some juvenile delinquent group of girls with a secret handshake. This is a well-organized criminal cult. They are a secret society that targets men of power and position, legal and illegitimate, but mainly illegal. And their influence is outstanding. They do not only operate and target individuals on a local level, they also have some of the nation's top cartels and crime families under their remote control. On every level, from the low-grade street dealers to the top bosses, they have managed to influence and manipulate their way into the underworld like law enforcement could never imagine doing themselves." McCarthy took a sip of his cup of cold coffee. "And they didn't just stop there. They're much smarter than that. They have done the same things with honest, hardworking citizens of power. Lawyers, judges, law enforcement." He let his words linger in the air before he continued. "They are now deeply rooted in the corporate world. Their white-collar crimes are on a scale like no other. Their schemes are both productive and effective."

"Exactly what methods are they using?" a different voice asked from the dark.

Agent McCarthy walked back to the podium and pressed a button and the lights came back on. He reluctantly answered, "This is exactly what I'm getting at. What we are up against is something like we've never seen before, or even encountered. It is a level of strong-armed blackmail that seems simplistic, but is really so far advanced. It's a webbing system that protects them like a fortress. And it all starts with an initiation process. So with each targeted victim, they get stronger.

"Their selections are far from random, for both recruit and the target. Both are thoroughly investigated and handpicked by a selective few gang members. Right now it is unclear how many. But we do know that they all report to one woman, that being Ms. Fields. And she may or may not be reporting to someone else, that being Queen Fem who, as I stated earlier, is a mystery. We do, however, know that they go after men of power, on both a low and high level, from drug dealers to politicians. But only those with the most to lose. They know exactly who's weak and, more importantly, who'll break. They learn exactly who has what to protect and how far they will go to do so. Then they go after it, through them. They get into isolated positions with their targets and use forcefully degrading acts to hang over their heads, according to my intel source. Now, here's the most brilliant part, which complicates things for us. Technically, they're clean. Everything about them checks out. Aside from their heat-packing motorcycle gang security branch, the rest of them appear to be high-class, law-abiding citizens with respectable jobs. They only get their hands dirty one time: the initiation process. Which means, technically, they aren't even a part of the Double Gs yet when they commit the actual criminal act."

"So why don't we just bring them down under the RICO Act or 848 CCE?" a uniformed DEA agent asked from his seat.

"Good question. But with what? All we'll get is a couple of misdemeanor gun charges, and circumstantial evidence of blackmail. It's hard to paint a clear picture to the jury for them to see what we're dealing with. Nothing will stick without successfully retrieving some hardcore evidence. Nothing," Agent McCarthy emphasized.

"So what about this Queen Fem? Any leads on her?" a special operative of the Secret Service inquired.

"None. She's been a ghost since the beginning of time. It seems that only Ms. Fields can lead us to her. But, until then, she's taking all the heat."

"You also say you have a source. Please specify?" the secretary of the Justice Department asked.

Agent McCarthy was hesitant to elaborate. His reluctance was evident. "Yes. I recently got an undercover agent inside who provides intel," he confirmed.

"Undercover?" the secretary asked.

"That is correct," Agent McCarthy confirmed.

"Did the agent also complete the initiation process? And is she also a lesbian?" a uniformed officer asked with a humorous undertone in his voice. A few officers chuckled, finding both questions to be tickling.

Agent McCarthy grew visibly agitated. "The necessary steps have been taken to get us on the inside. And to the next level," he declared.

"And what is the primary objective?" a Homeland Security officer asked from his front-row seat.

"Objective number one: finding Queen Fem or something solid. Second: take down and disassemble the Double Gs for good. We have to send a message to the others. A strong message!" Agent McCarthy banged his fist on the podium.

Each representative from the organizations looked back and forth at one another and then back at Agent McCarthy with agreeing nods. On the outside, Agent McCarthy was stone-faced, but on the inside he was smiling. *Step one: mission accomplished,* he thought.

"Now, gentlemen, let's get to work!"

Chapter Four

Anthony Frost lay back in the deluxe king-sized bed of his Villagio condo out in North Las Vegas, anxiously filled with excitement. *This that life right here. Shit don't get too much better than this*. He was convinced this would be an unforgettable evening. The low-playing tunes of Future filled his dimly lit condo's master bedroom. The setting was just right, he thought, but not nearly as perfect as he felt the situation was. He couldn't help but smile at what he believed was about to go down.

He folded his muscular arms behind his head and a light devilish grin spread across his hairless baby face. Although he didn't want to rush a single second, he couldn't wait for the night to be over so he could brag to his crew about the unfolding episode that was taking place. Wishing that they could share his current view, he selfishly went back to enjoying it all by himself. His dick stiffened from the two women's thickness. Breasts and ass protruded everywhere. Being a big man himself, there was nothing that turned him on more than a plus-size woman, and he was fortunate to have two.

Both women were nearly identical from top to bottom, with the exception of a birthmark on the chin of the darker one. Only five foot seven, their solid 200 pounds protruded in all the right places. Their double Ds looked as if they were fighting to break out of the Victoria's Secret bras and their asses nearly swallowed up the matching lace boy short panties they sported. The bottoms of their cheeks possessed a perfect cuff. Where the cuff ended, the full length of their muscular legs began. They stood at the foot of his bed and slow danced while they caressed one another.

Anthony licked his lips as he eyed their Amazonian builds. He didn't know exactly how to feel; it was weird to him at first, because they were obviously sisters. Twins in fact. But at the same time, it turned him on to see something so forbidden. Anthony just watched, waiting to see how far things would go between them. He had no way of knowing that the two sisters, who were born Gareesha and Nareesha Fowler, had been exploring each other's bodies playfully, then eventually in an incestuous manner, since they were little girls.

Sparkle had a mesmeric glaze in her eyes that was electrifying. She stared her mirror image, Glitter, in the face. They interlaced their fingers of both hands together and passionately slow danced to the music, grinding their bodies together in a soft, sensual manner.

Sparkle broke eye contact and turned around, pressing her back into Glitter's inner thighs. Glitter never stopped the rhythmic flow. She skillfully reached around to the front of Sparkle's thick waist and stuck her right hand into her panty line. Sparkle gasped, releasing a sexual sigh of relief as she rested the back of her head on Glitter's collarbone. They both decided to put on one hell of a show for their solo audience member. Glitter pulled her hand up and out of Sparkle's panties and stuck her glistening index finger into her own mouth, allowing her long, stiff tongue to swipe up her sister's honey nectar. She then turned her head to smile at Anthony, who was lying on top of his bed's silk Gucci sheets, dying for a piece of the action.

In sync, as rehearsed, both girls turned and climbed on top of the bed. They split up, one crawling on each side of his muscular frame. All Anthony could think about at that moment was how the twins claimed they didn't do penetration. But on the way home from Treasures, where they were employed, he knew that statement would soon be a thing of the past. At minimum, if that weren't the case, he figured he'd at least get a dynamic double blow job from two super thick twins. *This some real live fantasy shit at its best,* he thought. Still, he couldn't help but feel that it was all kinds of kinky.

His ill thoughts were interrupted by the touch of Sparkle stroking the right side of his chest while Glitter sucked on the left side of his neck. To heighten the mood, Glitter reached down into the crotch of Anthony's silk boxers and fondled his magic stick. She smiled at the fact that he was leaking pre-cum already. Anthony extended both of his arms. He rubbed both sisters' asses at the same time while they teased and pleasured his body. *Damn these muthafuckas thick as fuck.*

Sparkle pulled the right side of Anthony's face toward her to draw his attention more on her. They both locked eyes. Sparkle leaned in and bit his bottom lip. She then reached across his waist and stuck her right hand into her sister's panties the way Glitter had done to her earlier. She made sure to get her fingers nice and wet before pulling them back out. Glitter shut her eyes and moaned from her sister's touch as she breathed heavily into Anthony's ear. He was loving every second of it. Sparkle raised her soaked fingers up to her mouth. She stared at them seductively before sticking her tongue out and slowly licking the juice off her index finger with just the tip of her tongue. She then put them in front of Anthony's face.

"I've saved just enough for you, daddy," she softly whispered. Her fingers were so close that he could actually smell her sister's natural, sweet-smelling scent. He parted his lips and allowed her to place her two fingers into his mouth as he gently sucked off Sparkle's saliva and Glitter's vaginal secretions mixed together.

Glitter broke free of her own exotic trance. The drugs had her caught up in the moment, but she managed to snap back to reality. She jumped out of bed while making sure to catch eye contact with her sister before she spoke. "Now listen, baby. I know we've kept you waiting long enough, so we're going to freshen up a bit, and then when we return, trust me, you'll be in for the show of your life." Glitter licked her lips seductively.

He lay back and refolded his arms behind his head, still grinning. "Don't make me wait too much longer," he smoothly stated in a flirtatious, yet sarcastic, manner.

"Oh, we definitely won't," Sparkle reassured him as she rose up from beside him to join her sister at the foot of the bed. She grabbed her Michael Kors bag from the floor next to her clothes and met her sister's pace as they secretly giggled their way into the bathroom and shut the door behind them.

Glitter pulled out her makeup kit and opened it. She lightly poured the white powdered substance onto the bathroom sink. Sparkle had just finished rolling up the dollar bill she had pulled out of her bag into a quill. Glitter retrieved a card from her bag and separated the drug. Once she was done, Sparkle leaned down and sniffed the line closest to her until there was no more. She then took her pointer finger, pressed it down on the residue and then rubbed it across her teeth before licking her finger clean. Once she passed the quill to her sister, Glitter completed the same ritual. Sparkle then removed two pills from a small change purse. She handed one of the pills known as a molly to her sister and popped the other one into her mouth. They stared at one another and smirked. They had a way of communicating with facial expressions and silence. They both strolled out of the bathroom in seductive manners. Sparkle set her bag beside the nightstand this time and dug into it while Glitter climbed back into the bed with Anthony and straddled him.

Anthony was quite sure that the moment had arrived, so he grabbed a firm hold of Glitter's waist and positioned the crotch of her moist panties to land directly on top of his bulge in his boxers. He could feel the warmth penetrating through both of their thin fabrics. Glitter looked down at him and placed her hands on his rock-hard chest while shutting her eyes tight and licking her lips as she ground back and forth. Sparkle knew that it was the perfect time for her to join back in.

She slowly climbed back into the bed and sat with her feet tucked under her butt cheeks. Glitter held her position without reopening her eyes. She listened to what was going on as Anthony set his attention on her sister, who began to take over the show.

"Here's how this works. I guess you caught us off guard on a good night. Now, it's time for us to have some real fun," Sparkle declared.

Anthony lay on his back, staring up at the two gorgeous sisters. "I'm down fo' whateva," he whispered just above the music. "What y'all have in mind?"

Sparkle flashed a smile. "Just what I wanted to hear," she replied. She revealed two sets of steel handcuffs. Each pair was covered with blue and pink fur. The particular colors were chosen to make them appear less harmful.

Anthony cracked a forced smile as his eyes widened. "And what do y'all plan to do with those?" he asked in a cool manner.

Both Sparkle and Glitter smiled. Sparkle then began to pout like a little schoolgirl as she stuck her index finger into one of the handcuff's loops and let it dangle in front of him. "See, I thought you were one of the big boys, and look at the show we just put on for you tonight. You won't even let us have just a little fun," she whined playfully.

A frown appeared on Anthony's face. He shook his head to indicate he was not down for whatever the twins had in mind. He had done some freaky things in his sexual career, but being handcuffed had never been in the equation.

Sparkle rose up off the bed. Despite the air conditioner being on full blast, she began to fan herself. By now, the molly and the cocaine she had popped and sniffed began to take effect. It was no secret her sister had a higher tolerance than her and more patience. She became impatient with Anthony and irritated behind the situation. She shot Glitter a look that meant they could be spending their evening doing something far better than what they were doing at that moment. She was all too ready to abandon what they had started. Usually when she got high she wanted to be somewhere turned up. When that was the case, making money while having a good time went hand in hand. Tonight she knew that was not the case.

"C'mon, Glitter, let's be out of here!" Sparkle announced.

Glitter shot her sister a look back to try to calm her. Unlike Sparkle, Glitter did not want to end what they had started. She felt they had come too far to turn around now.

Anthony watched the exchange between the two sisters. He could feel he was just moments away from a dream come true turning into a nightmare. He swallowed the hard, dry lump in his throat as Sparkle repeated herself.

Anthony let out a loud sigh as Glitter began to rise up off the top of his rock-hard shaft. He looked down at the wet spot she had left on the crotch of his boxers. Some of the secretions had managed to transfer through onto the sensitive skin of his erect manhood.

"Yo, hold up," he pleaded. He couldn't just let them leave like that.

Sparkle and Glitter both stopped in their tracks and turned toward Anthony.

"Look, just don't put them shits on too tight,"
Anthony gave in. "I've been fighting hard not to
feel a pair of those ever again. Now, y'all got me
volunteering. Unfuckingbelievable." He cracked
a light chuckle to depressurize the mood.

Both girls glanced at each other. They couldn't
help but reveal huge smiles. Although it wasn't
planned, things could not have gone any better,
they thought. Sparkle and Glitter wasted no time
sliding on opposite sides of the bed. Sparkle
threw Glitter the pair of matching cuffs. They
both grabbed one of Anthony's wrists and cuffed
them to the brass loopholes in his bedpost.

The second Anthony felt restrained he regretted his consent. Although the cuffs weren't on
too tight, he realized that there wasn't any way
that he could get loose on his own. He tried to
make light of the situation. "Please tell me y'all
have the keys," he seriously joked.

"Of course we do, silly!" Sparkle laughed it off
as she and Glitter climbed back into the bed.

They both began kissing on him and rubbing
his chest again. Glitter caressed his sack. His
dick immediately shot back up. She ran one of
her fingers up and down his pulsating veins.
Sparkle could feel his heartbeat racing from
anticipation. She climbed up closer to her sister and stared into her eyes. A long, slow, and

passionate kiss began to transpire between the two of them as they fondled each other. It was as if they were caught up in a whirlwind of lust. They abruptly broke their lip lock and drew their attention to Anthony.

Sparkle held Glitter's arms while speaking directly to him. "Now, here is how this works. I know we told you we don't do penetration, but you were kind of right when you said, 'There's a first time for everything.'"

Anthony smiled as he looked back and forth at his restrained wrists before responding. "So, y'all gonna let me loose so that I can play too?" he questioned with a cocky grin.

Glitter decided to join the dialogue. "Of course you can play, daddy. In fact, we couldn't do it without you," she stated as she gripped a handful of his erection.

Sparkle joined in and grabbed his balls. "All you have to do now is choose which one of us you want," Sparkle declared as they held each other, staring at him.

Rather than choose, he opted to be greedy. "I want you both," he replied.

The twins were not surprised by his response. They both grinned at the other. Glitter freed her grip of her sister, crawled up on his chest and began to tongue kiss him with exaggerated desire. With every aggressive swirl of their tongues, Anthony yanked on his restraints, wishing he could touch her. But he couldn't. He was so caught up in the mood that he never even noticed Sparkle slip away back into the bathroom, only to reappear two minutes later, standing in front of the bed. When he finally saw her, his eyes bulged out of his head. He smiled as he felt he was in for a bigger treat than he had expected. He stared at the nine-inch strap-on dildo that Sparkle wore and he thought of how it couldn't get any better watching her fuck her own sister. *Yeah, loosen that pussy up for me before I get a hold of it.* His ego was on 1,000 at that moment.

As he began to run away with the brief fantasy, Glitter rose up from off of him and stood by her sister. They both began to giggle while they stared at him. Suddenly, the heat of passion disappeared and the room turned frigid. The twins now eyed him down like a piece of meat in front of two hungry wolves. The smile slowly slid from Anthony's face. For some strange reason, something didn't feel right to him.

"Yo, wassup?" Anthony questioned. His words came out alarmed and timid. Concern was written all over his face.

Sparkle and Glitter stood there with sinister grins on their faces. The drug had them charged up and they were ready to turn up the heat. "I guess I'll go first, Glitter," Sparkle proclaimed.

"Yeah, go ahead, be my guest, sis," Glitter replied as she strolled over to the nightstand that Sparkle set her Michael Kors bag near.

A sense of panic swept through Anthony's body. "Uh uh! What the fuck? I ain't into all of that extra freaky shit!" he aggressively yelled. "Let me the fuck loose!" he demanded in an authoritative tone.

The empty order fell upon deaf ears. In fact, things began to get even worse. He heard a familiar clicking sound that he knew all too well. He slowly turned toward Glitter's direction. She was pointing a chrome Desert Eagle right at his forehead.

"What the fuck? Oh, so y'all don't know who the fuck I am," he boasted as if everything was under full control. "Y'all just gonna come up in here and shit and think y'all gonna rob me?" he added.

The twins simply giggled.

"Calm down, daddy. We know exactly who you are. And no, we didn't come here to rob you for your money. The picture is so much bigger than that. However, we are goin' to take something from you that you can't get back." Sparkle explained as she began stroking the length of the strap-on as if it was her own stiff penis.

Anthony began to sweat profusely. "What? What type of shit y'all—"

Before he could finish his sentence, Glitter gun butted him so hard that the left side of his forehead split. He was instantly unconscious. After the twins made sure he wasn't faking, they uncuffed him and repositioned him again before recuffing him.

Glitter stepped back and grabbed the second item that was hidden behind Sparkle's Michael Kors bag. It was a video camcorder. She turned it on and scrolled through the menu. She aimed it at the target until live footage of him appeared on the screen. She pressed her record button and gave Sparkle a smile and head nod. The target was stabilized. It was finally time to execute the order.

Ten minutes later, Sparkle pressed stop on the camcorder and pause on the cell phone video recorder she was given, as Glitter stepped away from the unconscious figure, lying chained face flat on the bed. She reached for his silk boxers and used them to wipe herself off as she walked over to her sister.

"I guess he was right: we do do penetration," Sparkle sarcastically joked about the sodomizing act she had just committed. They both laughed at the irony of the situation.

"Sparkle, go 'head, send the video and call the number they gave us," Glitter suggested.

Sparkle scrolled through the phone's menu and texted the explicit raw footage to the anonymous number they had received along with the information on the target and the mission.

The twins impatiently paced the floor for a full fifteen minutes before the phone began vibrating. They both put their ears to the receiver and listened without saying a word as a soft but dominant voice came through.

"Okay, girls, good job. Y'all are in," the woman announced. "Be sure to return the camcorder where you retrieved it from."

The twins looked at one another, drowned in confusion. "That's it? Just like that? What do we do now?" Sparkle asked, not sure of what the next move was.

"About what?" the woman questioned.

"About him," Glitter intervened.

"Oh please. Do excuse me. It's been a long night for all three of us. Why don't you leave that to me. I'll take care of him right now. I assume he's still out cold and restrained. Correct?"

"Yeah, but I think he's coming to. He's starting to move," Glitter panicked.

The woman chuckled. "Good. Smack him around a li'l bit to wake him up, and then put me on speakerphone and hold it next to his ear."

The twins glanced at each other again. At that point they were just ready to get their belongings, leave, and just run from the consequences forever. They had just violated a very powerful man in the worst way and they weren't sure of how they would be protected from him. Still, they knew they had to finish what they had started.

"Nigga, wake up!" Sparkle smacked Anthony's right cheek repeatedly until he came to.

Anthony's eyes shot open. He looked around in a confused manner. He thought it was all just a bad dream. His vision was blurry and he felt dizzy. He then realized that he couldn't get up. His wrists were still cuffed to the bedrail. The burning sensation registered in the lower half of his body. Blood trickled down from his forehead into his left eye. He squinted hard, trying to focus his right pupil on his violators. He could barely speak from his throat drying up.

"Wh . . . Wha . . . What the fuck did y'all do to me?" He slowly struggled to finish the rhetorical question, not really wanting to know the answer.

He couldn't even remember if he was awake for it all, but the sharp pain shooting through his anus retold the story of exactly what happened. An unfamiliar voice entered his left ear.

"Hello, Mr. Frost, or should I address you by your street moniker?" The voice let out a light chuckle. It was more of a statement than a question. "Anyway, this is the leader of the Double G organization. Maybe you've heard of us, maybe you haven't, but we are a well-known resistance group of the underworld. And we are well protected. You have just been part of an initiation process by these two young ladies. They are now under our umbrella. We are responsible for them and their well-being. So, please, before you think about any type of retaliation, do your research on us first. You will find that there are many just like you who have been targeted and then forced to become our allies if ever we need assistance of any kind. If you weren't considered to be a useful asset to our organization then we wouldn't be having this conversation, because you'd be dead already.

"I am very aware of your power, and exactly what you are capable of. I also know your limits and, more importantly, your reach. And that's where we are up on you. You are restricted. Local. We are spread throughout the entire nation. We are everywhere you can think of or even imagine. And, everywhere we are, there are dozens like you who are forced to deal with us, even though they despise who we are, what we do, what we are about and, even more importantly, what we have done."

"Get to the fuckin' point!" Anthony grunted into the receiver.

"Okay. Have it your way. Here's the deal. I have live footage of what just took place. It is stored away in a computer file along with hundreds of others. If you choose to retaliate or show resistance in any kind of way, shape, form, or fashion, you will be killed. But only after we finish stripping you of everything and every person you love or even care about. And, on top of all that, the footage will be played at your funeral. Copies will be handed out to everyone throughout the entire Las Vegas area connected or associated with you. Your crew will spit on your name. Your legacy will be tarnished and reduced to dirt. And all you would be known for is being a has-been gangsta who got killed 'cause he fucked with the wrong bitches and got fucked!"

The phone went dead in his ear, and seconds later a text came through. Both girls read it aloud at the same time: "Keep this phone on at all times. Uncuff him and leave the memo on the bed for him, delete this text, and get outta there. Welcome to the family."

As instructed, Sparkle immediately deleted the text message. Glitter walked over toward the bed and uncuffed him and then tossed the white envelope at him. "This is for you," she dryly remarked.

"Fuck you, dyke bitch!" he spat. Sharp pains shot through his wrists from the handcuffs as he attempted to lash out at Glitter.

"No, more like fuck you, sweetie." Glitter smiled. "Welcome to the gay society. Faggot."

They both let out a thunderous laughter as they waved their good-byes and made their way out of Anthony Frost's bedroom.

Chapter Five

Starr hung up the phone and pushed herself back from the round table. The rest of the Double Gs rotated blunts around the room and sipped on assorted flavors of Cîroc, Hennessy, Rémy, and Patrón while they listened to Starr lay the law down to their latest victim. They were used to watching their leader in action, but it had been a minute since she had called an emergency meeting. All of the members were all too curious to know the nature of the unexpected gathering. Starr took a swig of the Peach Cîroc on the rocks with no chaser as she studied the faces and body language of her crew while they waited for the final member to arrive.

Under any other normal circumstances she would not have been the least bit concerned about her crew member's tardiness, because she was used to it, but tonight was different. The call she had received still weighed heavy on her mental. Tonight everybody was a suspect. She couldn't help but watch the people in the room she considered family, sisters, with a questionable and suspicious eye. She knew calling the emergency meeting would have all of them on high alert and that's exactly what she wanted. At that moment no one was exempt from the accusation she received from the anonymous caller. Starr's train of thought was interrupted by the sudden presence of her friend of seven years.

"Sorry I'm late again, everybody. My bad," Bubbles announced with a smile and wave. She peered nervously over at Starr. Seeing that her boss wasn't smiling, Bubbles wiped the smile off her face and replaced it with a more solemn, apologetic one. It was apparent to her that Starr was pissed or irritated by something. Aside from Starr being her boss, she was her closest friend and knew, even when others didn't, when Starr was bothered by something. Bubbles wasted no time finding her seat at the head of the round table next to Diamond and Felicia. All three looked at one another wide-eyed and shrugged.

Now that everyone was in attendance, Starr took her drink and tossed it back until her glass was empty. She then walked over to the table, scooped up two ice cubes, and picked up the half-gallon bottle of Peach Cîroc and refilled her glass. She put the drink up to her lips and drank half of the liquor.

Her actions instantly drew the attention of the other Double Gs. They all went from curious to uneasy. It wasn't too often that they saw their leader toss drinks back like that. They all knew the only time she actually did drink excessively was when either they were celebrating or there was a problem. Each woman voted on the latter and tightened up. Both blunts and drinks ceased as the members of the Double Gs sat attentively waiting for Starr to fill them in on why they were all there.

Starr took a deep breath. She chose her words wisely before she spoke. She could feel the sweet-tasting alcohol starting to kick in. She raised her head and sniffed the air. "Y'all smell that?" she asked the room.

Everybody in the room began to sniff the air and stare at each other with confused looks plastered across their faces. Starr knew they didn't and couldn't smell what she did, unless they were the cause of the foul stench.

"In case you can't smell it, I'll tell you what it is." A sinister grin appeared on Starr's face.

Everybody waited, eager to know what their leader smelled that they couldn't, outside of weed and liquor.

"I smell some bullshit!" she boomed out of nowhere.

Her words caused a few of the Double Gs to chuckle.

"Oh, you think shit funny?"

The sight of Starr's black nine millimeter cocking back was enough to cease all giggles and snickers. The room was filled with surprised looks. No one was surprised that Starr had drawn her weapon because it was a known fact that she was a certified shooter. They were surprised that she felt she needed to draw it in the room to prove a point. There was not a body in attendance that wouldn't lay or hadn't laid their life on the line for her or the crew.

Starr knew as soon as she drew her gun she had gone too far, but her emotions had gotten the best of her. She knew what was going on in everybody's mind, but at that moment she didn't care. There was a strong possibility that someone in the room jeopardized or compromised their organization and she wasn't having it. *Extreme measures for an extreme situation,* she told herself. *One of these bitches think it's a game, but I'm about to show them just how real it is.* She was now in a zone. She was in pure boss mode.

Felicia's voice brought her back. "Baby girl, what's the deal?" she asked.

Starr shook her head in disgust. "The deal is I got an anonymous call from some muthafucka sayin' we got an informant in our camp."

The word "informant" caused murmurs and chatter among the members of the Double Gs. Starr noticed the heads of everybody in the room shaking to indicate that they weren't who she was referring to. The scenery made Starr regret blurting the word out. She had trusted these women for years. There was no one in the room who hadn't been a Double G for at least three years while the rest had five and better by her side, without so much as a eyebrow raised at their loyalty. The room was in an uproar as surprised looks turned into offended ones. Starr knew she had to say something to gain order within the room.

"Look, I'm not pointing the finger at anybody, but I can't excuse the fact that it was thrown out there." Her words eased the room a bit. "Now, this shit can't be taken lightly. It's not a joking matter. If there's any truth to it, if one goes, we all go, so I'm sure you can understand my concern and anger." She let her words linger and marinate. "It's not just about me, it's about us. Double Gs for life. We ride or die and if somebody jeopardizes what we stand for, even if we embraced them as a Double G, they get rode on!" Starr's words triggered an uproar of agreement.

She watched the reaction of every member. *How the fuck can it be any of my sisters?* Every face seemed genuine in the room. They all had disapproving looks of a snitch being among the ranks and they were in agreement with riding for and with Starr.

"What about one of the probationers?" Bubbles pointed out.

Her statement brought silence into the room. No one, not even Starr, had given that any thought. It was as though a new light had been shed on the situation. Starr nodded and flashed an apologetic smile that only Bubbles managed to catch before she spoke.

"How many rookies we got on probation?" Starr directed the question to Felicia, who was in charge of initiations.

"Um, including the twins and the new boot I'm settin' up now, six."

"That means we got six potential snitches in our motherfuckin' camp," Diamond spat. She rolled her eyes in Starr's direction. She was pissed, but maintained her composure up until now. She wondered if her lover suspected her. It all made sense to her now why Starr had just up and left the other morning.

"True," Starr agreed. "But not necessarily true," she added. She noticed Diamond's attitude toward her and excused it. She knew what had fueled it.

"Fee, I need you to double back and do a more thorough check on them chicks to see if we overlooked something. Meanwhile, I'll run this pass Queen."

Felicia nodded.

"I know it's late so I'm not gonna prolong this meeting any further, so let me say this. I deeply and sincerely hope that nobody—and I put emphasis on the word—in this room has broken the code and gone against the grain." She let her words linger in the air before she continued. "Because, I love you all like my own flesh and blood. But if I am right, I promise you, God Almighty Himself will not be able to save you. That is all." She banged her fist on the table as she ended abruptly.

No one uttered a word. Instead they all rose and one by one they began to exit the room. Ten minutes later, the room only consisted of Starr, Diamond, Felicia, and Bubbles, and an additional meeting was held.

Chapter Six

Prime, also known as the Prime Minister, for ruling the streets with an iron fist, was a well-known figure all throughout the city of Las Vegas. He earned his name by being a very diplomatic person. He was either the perfect friend or the worst enemy. There was no in-between with him. A person always knew exactly where they stood with him. He was definitely a man of respect and exercised his power strategically. That made him a hard target; that and the fact that he was rarely ever seen. The only time he really stuck his neck out in public was when he was at his favorite spot relaxing and unwinding with his crew.

Prime loved the energy in Treasures. It was the only place he really liked showing up to show out at. He took pleasure in squandering his money in the establishment. He loved watching the women go crazy when he made it thunderstorm in the club with the bricks of singles, fives, tens, and twenties he would have the club manager bring him. While others tipped and took women to the VIP room and maxed out their credit cards on lap dances, Prime and his crew tossed enough money in the air in a single night to pay rent for every dancer in the club for at least six months. Although it was against the rules and forbidden, usually the night always ended the same after Prime and his crew turned up and balled out in the club. Many of the dancers would rush to get dressed and pack up their belongings so they could pile up in the convoy of luxury cars Prime and his crew had parked outside. There was no reason to think that tonight would be any different.

"So then what happened?" Prime asked with a blatant sarcastic smile, not believing a word of what he was hearing. He and his crew were up on the second floor in their personal VIP section. It was a section that had been solidified by them for the longest.

Young Clips continued the story that everyone knew he was concocting as he went along. They wondered if he actually ever realized it. "So, yeah, anyways, I got the bitch up in my ride.

We was kissin' 'n' shit and I'm feelin' all on her titties 'n' shit. I stuck my hand down her pants and started fingerin' her. She started goin' crazy, busting off right then and there." Young Clips grew more excited as he told his alleged tale.

"Hold up!" C-Class interrupted, while laughing over the music, along with everyone else. "You mean, Felicia? Felicia, Felicia?" he asked with extra sarcasm in his tone.

Young Clips instantly became pissed off. C-Class was ruining both his story and what he believed to be his shine, he thought. But nobody else believed him. Not even Prince, who was known for being the simple one out of the crew.

"Yeah, Felicia. She a stone-cold freak! I twisted her out right there on the spot," Young Clips added.

"Whateva, nigga! It's a well-known fact that Felicia is a stone-cold dike. And no disrespect, homie, but you ain't getting enough paper to make her want to change her mind!" C-Class retorted. The rest of the crew snickered and joined one another in laughter.

Young Clips was the youngest member of the crew. He had been accepted into the crew because he was a live wire and, most importantly, loyal. His gun constantly went off and he was also the leader of his own little team of younger, wilder gunslingers who only looked up to him because he was in Prime's crew.

C-Class and Young Clips went back and forth, while Prime was off in a daze. His focus was on the beautiful woman who sat at the bar. He noticed they had made eye contact as she sipped on her drink. He studied her and sized her up. *Nice,* he thought. He believed he was good at reading people and something about her look told him she had a hell of a story behind her. Prime excused himself from the VIP booth and made his way over in her direction. His crew watched as he glided out of their section and down to the public bar. Once they realized his destination, they resumed their conversation and drinks.

Finally, thought Monica. After attending Treasures every Friday for the past six months, she was more than confident that this night would be the moment she had been waiting for. She sat at the bar with her legs crossed and scanned the crowd while she awaited the female bartender to service her. Many times, guys would approach her, but she brushed them off politely. She needed to stay focused and, more importantly, alone. *Don't blow it,* she reminded herself. *Play your cards right tonight and the reward will be worth the risk,* she reasoned.

As the months passed, she had gotten to know more and more about the Double Gs. Through observing, listening, and being shown, she had pretty much learned the normal flow of operation of the organization. But tonight was something different. This was officially her first mission. This could make or break her. The thought of it had Monica on pins and needles.

The bartender finally emerged and made her way over to Monica and smiled. Monica recognized her immediately. She had first seen her outside Club Panties the night Felicia had gotten into it with the female security guard. She saw her again inside the club. She remembered her being among the group of Double Gs who sported their organization's club colors. They danced and chanted together to their favorite songs.

The bartender leaned in closer to Monica and propped her elbows on the countertop. "And how may I help you?"

Monica returned the smile, and a bit of nervousness swept throughout her entire body. She took a deep breath to help calm her nerves. The last thing she wanted to do was blow her chance before it came. She pretended not to recognize the bartender. She got into character.

"Umm. I would like a blue martini, with two lemons, one lime, no ice, and an umbrella straw." It was an order that she had rehearsed for a month before she had ever entered the establishment.

Since Felicia had recruited her, she was responsible for Monica. She made sure Monica was clear on the specific order and knew what she had to do. Monica knew the drink order all too well. She often dreamt about placing the order in her sleep.

Apparently, the bartender was quite familiar with it also. She raised back upright. She flashed an even broader smile. "Okay. Comin' right up. Ummm, will that be all?" she vibrantly asked.

"For now," Monica boldly stated. Her butterflies began to settle. The bartender nodded and then disappeared.

Monica spun her rotating stool around and faced the lounge section. She watched everyone who was indulging in various forms of entertainment. She evaluated every person she laid eyes on. She couldn't help but feel as if she, herself, was being watched. She knew she was from both sides at that. It was the whole point.

Within a matter of minutes, the bartender returned with the drink. She made sure to catch Monica's full attention before dropping the professional smile and making stern eye contact.

She slid Monica a small hand-sized drawstring pouch. Monica noticed it had something of weight inside of it. The quick transaction seemed to go unnoticed as Monica slipped it into her Gucci bag. She then rose up from the barstool and made her way to the ladies' room without even paying for her drink. She was quite sure it was complimentary. Once she had reviewed and secured the content, she returned to where she had been posted up for most of her evening in the club. Less than five minutes after returning to the bar, she detected movement and a sudden presence approaching out of her right side periphery. She took a short breath and put on her game face.

When Prime reached the female at the bar, he did a quick scan and took her appearance all in. She stood and greeted him with a welcoming smile. Prime nodded. The first thing he noticed was how her almond skin glistened creating a golden tint to her complexion. It reminded him of Taral Hicks, who played Keisha in the movie *Belly*. Her nose was small and round. Her eyes were wide and almond shaped. Her lips were small but full with bright red lipstick on them. Her hair was cut in an old-school Halle Berry style. But what stood out the most was her physique. She was cornbread thick, just the way he liked them. He played her natural height for five foot nine or ten, but her stilettos made her appear taller. She was between 190 and 200 pounds, give or take, but she wore it in all the right places well, he noticed.

There is nothing like a full-figured, sexy-ass black woman, thought Prime. Any imagination could capture just how explosive her thick, curvaceous body was. Her breasts illuminated at the top of her red strapless, form-fitting Dior dress. The dress hugged her tight waist and stopped just past her protruding hips, making her ass appear 3D. It sat up and out enough to set a drink or two on it. Prime was impressed. It was evident to him that she had class, and an independent aura about herself: other traits Prime was attracted to. Prime stood directly in front of her. He leaned over on the bar right beside her and motioned for the bartender.

The bartender flashed him a smile and came right over. "What's up, Prime?" she asked, knowing that he rarely ever came over to that particular section.

"Ain't nothin'. Give me another two rounds of whatever she's having," he requested, never taking his eyes off the mysterious woman in the red dress.

The bartender scurried to fill Prime's order.

The girl smiled at Prime. "Are you trying to get me drunk?" she flirtatiously asked with a seductive grin she appeared to be trying to hold back.

Prime smiled back at her. "Nah. You look like a big girl, and I mean that as a compliment, who can hold her own, without getting into anything she can't handle." He flashed a Colgate smile. "I'm just tryin'a get *you*, period." He backed his smile up with a wink.

She blushed. "You got a name?" she asked.

"Yeah. Prime. Yours?"

"Monica," she replied. "But people call me Moe."

Just then, the bartender returned with the drinks and set them between the two of them then backpedaled away out of earshot of their conversation.

Meanwhile, Freeze sat in a separate VIP section on the opposite side of Treasures. He popped bottles of rosé and assorted flavors of Cîroc with his crew. They were known for being much wilder in the streets than most of the squads that were Treasures's regulars. They also had their own private booth that was exclusively reserved for them whenever they entered the luxurious establishment.

Like Prime and his crew, Freeze's group popped bands and tossed stacks of money into the air nonstop. They poured out and sprayed more champagne than they actually drank, as the exotic dancers rotated performances for them.

Tonight, Freeze had been more laidback than usual. He had a lot on his mind. He sat and listened partially as his team openly discussed many topics, mostly about business. He was receiving a full report after not being around for an entire week.

"So, we took care of them niggas up the hill. They won't be giving us no more static. They know they have no other choice but to move out. And they can only get their work from us. We basically only have to worry about them jokers over there, and we got shit locked," Esco declared, while pointing directly over to Prime's crew.

For some reason, Freeze seemed distant to Esco. He was used to his boss's feedback, but he noticed he hadn't really been in any of the previous conversations that his crew was indulging in. Esco tried to switch it up, making light conversation.

"But fuck them dudes! Our plan is almost in full effect. On the other side of things though,"

Esco said, and leaned in closer and smiled harder, "holla at ya boy. You ain't even fill me in on what happened with you and them two thick-ass twins you took home from here last week. I don't see them in here tonight. Give me the rundown."

Freeze's eyes grew cold as his face turned to stone. He simply stared back at Esco. He tried to conceal how the question had immediately rubbed him the wrong way before his flared nostrils gave him away. He pretended not to hear Esco's question and didn't bother to reply. The last thing he wanted to talk about was the night that had officially forever changed life as he once knew it. He still couldn't believe he had gotten caught slipping. There was no way he could ever let something like what had happened to him get out. There was no one he could confide in, not even his right-hand man, Esco. He was sure he and anyone else would look at him differently. He knew he would not be respected the way he was now by his crew and in the streets, and he had to do everything in his power to ensure that it didn't get out. The thought of it infuriated Freeze the more he thought about it. The incident was still fresh, but he was already contemplating his next move on how he intended to handle the matter.

The night was coming to an end as bodies poured out of Treasures. Freeze and his crew made their way out of the club. They couldn't help but notice Prime's crew posted up in their VIP section surrounded by a dozen or more of some of Vegas's finest.

"Look at them niggas over there frontin'. I'm ready to give it to them right now," Esco barked, gripping the Glock in his waist. His speech was somewhat slurred. The liquor had long ago taken effect on him and was now doing the talking.

He had been in Freeze's ear all night about Prime's crew. Watching them ball out frustrated him. One would say he was actually hating on Prime and his crew, but Esco would beg to differ. Normally Freeze wouldn't have been so easily influenced, but after what he endured, he was up for a good testosterone challenge. It was just what he needed to restore the feeling of manly power that he had lacked since his run-in with the twins.

"Word. Let's go see how they actin'. Right here. Right now. They're in our way. It's time to move them," Freeze declared.

That was exactly what Esco wanted to hear all night. He took one last swig of the bottle of Red Berry Cîroc he had been taking to the head the entire night and then slammed it down on the table. His nostrils flared and his facial expression transformed into a deadly one.

Freeze detoured and made a beeline in the direction of Prime's crew. Esco, along with the rest of the wolves, followed.

Prime was still at the bar sealing the deal with Monica. He had been whispering in her ear, telling her everything that she had wanted to hear since he had met her. When the music abruptly stopped, Prime's danger alarm immediately went off. He turned and looked and noticed the sudden commotion in the direction of his VIP section.

"Fuck," Prime cursed.

Young Clips had been the first to jump up and pull out his twin .44s, aiming them directly at Esco, who had his own pistol aimed at Prince and C-Class.

C-Class remained sealed with a smile on his face as if everything was under control. Prince showed much more frustration but stayed calm. Young Clips wasn't having it. He ignored the screaming and remained focused.

The bartender saw the potential altercation unfolding and got on the phone immediately. Prime watched her and assumed she was calling the police. That was the last thing he needed.

Prime knew he had to react quickly. He wasted no time heading over to his crew.

Esco and Young Clips were locked in a stand-off, neither about to lower their weapons. Instead, their fingers tightened around the triggers of their weapons, eager to squeeze. Security stood at bay. They were familiar with both crews and thought it best to stay out of the mix. It was they who had actually allowed the crews in with their guns in exchange for healthy tips.

Freeze played the background. His frustration grew from the distraction of the continuous vibration of his cell phone, which he sent straight to voicemail three times. The fourth time forced him to retrieve his phone from his hip clip. He became irritated when he glanced at the screen.

Surprisingly, the woman followed right behind Prime, showing no fear, although she was highly uncomfortable with what was taking place. She stayed by his side the whole time as he strolled over to the ruckus in a nonchalant manner. He walked directly in between Esco's and Young Clips's weapons. Esco's barrel was aimed at his chest and Young Clips's gun was pointed at his back. Prime locked eyes with Esco.

"Is there a problem here? I'm sure we can settle it elsewhere," he calmly stated with an authoritative tone.

Just then, the owner of Treasures came running out of his back office with fear and infuriation mixed. He kept his distance, paying more attention to the frantic private dancers who were panicking as they ran to the back dressing room. Most of the customers were long gone after the music stopped and the first gun had been cocked.

Freeze hung up his phone as he sped up to the side of Esco. He placed his hand over the Glock and pushed it downward until it was pointing at the ground. He smiled at the woman in the red dress.

"Freeze, wassup?" Esco challenged.

Freeze ignored Esco. His eyes dimmed as he refocused them on Prime.

"You're right. And this must be your lucky night. Another time, another place. Come on, fellas!" He reached in his pocket and pulled out a knot of cash. He peeled off thirty hundred-dollar bills, dropped them into the champagne bucket on the nearest table, and then stepped off.

His frustrated crew trailed behind him. They had never seen Freeze back down from a fight. Especially one that they felt was won before it started.

Prime and his crew watched as Freeze and his cronies made their exit. Prime's crew spoke among themselves about what they could've and should've done. But they were used to Prime using intellect over emotions and more stealth and strategy than public outbursts and unnecessary gunplay.

As the last man left, the woman in the red dress was more than relieved. She grabbed a hold of Prime's hand as if she had known him forever. Due to the fact that he respected her fearlessness, he embraced her.

Although C-Class and Prince knew that Prime had done the right thing by trying to defuse the situation, they still wanted revenge. They had never been publicly challenged in such a way. The beef was on.

As Prime and the woman stepped outside the club, she looked at the rest of his crew. She was disappointed that the night he had promised her had turned into a blown one. *Better luck next time,* she thought. She reached into her purse and handed him a card with her number on it.

Prime gently pushed it away. "I'll get it from you in the morning," he declared with a smile.

She blushed, knowing it was an indirect invitation for her to spend the night with him. Within minutes, she was in the passenger seat of Prime's pearl white Aston Vanquish. He was outside talking to C-Class about what the next move should be. She had just ended her text and was powdering her nose when Prime hopped in the driver seat of his Aston.

The bartender couldn't believe the close call that she had previously witnessed. She nervously wondered how the rest of the night would play out. As she stood behind the bar, wiping it down, preparing to get off work, her hip vibrated. It had to be the call she was waiting for. She cautiously looked both ways before unclipping her phone and opening it up. She anxiously read the text that came through. It was from the phone that she had given Monica earlier when she first entered the bar and ordered the secret code drink.

The bartender sighed from relief as she forwarded the text message to Starr.

Chapter Seven

Meanwhile, less than a quarter of a mile up the street, Club Panties was jumping. Beautiful women spilled in and out nonstop. While they were enjoying themselves, below them more important things were taking place; the members of the Double Gs held their monthly meeting in the secret sublevel, in what was called the Ovary Office. This was the office that usually only the four of them were privy to. It was located one floor up from the general Double G meeting room. Starr was the only one standing. The rest of the Double Gs were all sitting. Tonight was different from the random and regular meetings they had. This was the meeting where all members reported monthly earnings, progress on any missions, introduction of any new Double Gs and whatever else Starr wanted to discuss. It was a mandatory requirement of Starr's for them all to wear their club's colors during monthly meetings. Each vest possessed a number on it that represented when they had become a Double G. Some of the vests also displayed unique patches that acknowledged skills such as sharpshooting or represented bravery. Starr ran the operation like a military camp by using ranking and special skills. It was a way of instilling discipline, responsibility, structure, and pride within her comrades.

Looking at Starr, you couldn't tell that she was in her early thirties, nor would you think she was as ruthless as she had proven to be in the past. Her soft-spoken voice and appearance made her seem somewhat timid, but that was far from being the case. Starr was a beautiful beast at five foot eleven and 220 pounds. She had a light caramel complexion, with long jet-black silky hair that dangled down to the middle of her back. She had deep, chinky eyes, with long lashes. Her eyebrows looked as if they were drawn on with a pencil. At a young age, she was aware of her big-boned physique. She learned the power of the female body early and worked vigorously on her full figure to get it where it was today. Over the years it had paid off and then some. Starr's curvy body sat perfectly inside of her black cat suit that fit like a glove. She stood in front of the organization she had helped shape into what it was today.

The Double Gs. Diamond, who was half Philippine and half Ethiopian, sat beside Starr. Her face was emotionless. Her deep chocolate face was nearly covered by the True Religion cap she sported low, with the exception of her petite Asian nose and glossy, full African lips. All the other Double Gs sat awaiting the monthly meeting to start. Although there was someone over her, as far as they were all concerned Starr was their boss.

One of the things that made Starr the face of the organization was the fact that she was the only one who was ever in direct contact with the infamous, yet anonymous, Queen Fem.

From what was told to her by Queen Fem, the Double Gs had originally started the organization as a means of revenge, but it grew to become so much more. According to her, she managed to recruit a group of women who were done with men, and set out against any one of them in power, position, or both. Over the early years, it evolved into a secret infiltration group that conned men out of whatever assets the original Double Gs needed for forward progress and expansion. Then Starr came along. With her at the helm, the Double Gs became a franchised criminal dynasty. Her love and passion for motorcycles added a new flavor to their rough persona, and a valuable tool to their already dangerous reputation. On many occasions, the machines had been used to execute strategic instructions given by Starr.

After a while, learning how to ride became a mandatory requirement if you were chosen to be a Double G. Although she wasn't the founder, hands down it was no secret who the boss was. Starr's methods of handling things and the way she ran the crew had put her in harm's way on many occasions, but everyone knew that it was her knowledge of the original founder that was the leverage that was keeping her alive and two sometimes three steps ahead of the authorities.

Queen Fem was a mysterious person, whose arms reached further than any of them knew. Everyone wanted to know who she was and how to get to her. She was like an old folktale. A ghost. A myth. No one from the newer generation had ever dealt with her directly or met her personally. Queen Fem had long ago passed on the torch of running the organization to Starr. Outside of conference calls and memos she sent out to the Double Gs and targeted victims, and the fact that she was the one in possession of all of the G-Files, as they called them, none of the Double Gs in attendance would even know that Queen Fem really existed. Everything that went on was stored and sent directly to her. The Double Gs learned their history about Queen Fem through Starr. Everyone had a picture of a sophisticated but ruthless woman. Whoever tried to search for her got dealt with. It was said that you didn't look for Queen Fem; she found you. That went for both sexes. There was a lot of speculation and it was rumored that Starr and Queen Fem were one and the same, but that couldn't be further from the truth. They were indeed two totally different individuals.

"We got a lot to discuss tonight," Starr opened up with as she looked around at the organization's members. On the table in front of her sat an electronic device.

Stone faces filled the room. Felicia, Diamond, and Bubbles, who were her closest allies, sat around the table, while the others lined the walls and occupied the available chairs scattered throughout the room. As Starr continued to take in all the faces in the room, her eyes zeroed in on Glitter and Sparkle, who sat beside each other by the entrance of the meeting room. She had a strong feeling recruiting the twins would prove to be a major move from the organization. She had big plans and tonight she intended to play chess with her crew. She had to make sure everybody on her team was rock solid before she could move forward. It had been over a week since she had received the anonymous call and she was still bothered by it. She couldn't afford any slipups or mishaps. There was a lot at stake, not only for her but for everyone. She believed it was her responsibility to see to it that nothing or no one could come and infiltrate the Double G organization. Tonight she intended to observe all the pieces in attendance to see if pawns had to be sacrificed and removed.

"I need everybody in this room to take this polygraph," she announced, pointing down at the lie detector as she monitored the rest of the Double Gs' faces.

Chapter Eight

Although Freeze was only twenty-seven, he had already made a dent in the streets. He relentlessly lived up to his notorious handle, "Freeze." His cold demeanor and heart showed time and time again whenever a situation arose. Aside from the Double Gs getting to him, he seemed virtually untouchable. He thrived on being exposed, out in the open. He was well known for putting in work himself. Most of the time he preferred it that way and his team was just as relentless. Some members of his crew were older than him, but a lot were younger, wilder, upcoming gangsters with smoking guns trying to prove themselves and make a name in the process. Still, at all times, it remained quite lucid that Freeze was the general.

Not only did Freeze have the muscle, but he also had the brains. Besides being street literate, he also took self-education to a whole other level. He never got a fair chance at finishing school. His main focus was providing for him and his younger sister. Aside from hitting the streets, he still looked over his old textbooks and deciphered the lessons in them. He loved figuring things out, especially math. Algebra was his favorite. He could answer any question right off the top of his head. He was intrigued by mental challenges, such as puzzles and riddles. He was quite a serious kid, but he was a pure mentalist. It was a side of him that he kept to himself. The rest of the world only saw him one way: maliciously sinister. Let him tell it, his rough childhood rightfully allowed him to claim to be a product of his environment.

Unlike most of his peers, Freeze started out his life with both of his parents in the picture. Freeze was the product of Marlon Frost, an infamous gangster known throughout the entire West Coast, and Monique Frost, a stay-at-home wife from North Las Vegas, who knew nothing about the streets other than the fact that her husband loved them. His father was known for making lots of money in the underworld and having a asshole full of women at his disposal. He ran a clockwork operation out of two public housing developments on opposite sides of the city, using females on welfare apartments. He strategically kept two different types of heroin grades in each one, so that the two buildings constantly competed against each other. He would masterfully maneuver the clientele back and forth across town. The steady competition between both sides drew unbelievable income. Most of the time, his father stayed out in the streets, laid up with other women, while Freeze's mother was at home raising him and his baby sister. He and Freeze never bonded. When he was home, Freeze mostly stayed in his room as a means to avoid him. When their paths did cross in the hallway or in passing, there was always an awkward silence between them.

Freeze just never really liked him too much. His mother always said it was because they were so much alike in so many ways. Freeze used to listen to his mother and father fight nearly every night about his father staying out and traveling so much. Freeze hated the way his father treated his mother. He had wished on many occasions that his father never returned home once he walked out of the front door. One day, his wish became a harsh reality. Freeze was barely nine years old, but the day was so vivid. He and his six-year-old sister were sitting at the dinner table with their mother. The phone had rung. Their mother excused herself and leaned over the kitchen counter to answer the call. She picked up, listened, and didn't utter a word. Freeze noticed his mother's jaw dropped.

Both Freeze and his sister watched as their mother covered her open mouth with her hands, letting the phone drop to the floor. Shortly after, her body collapsed right beside it. She was unable to take the news that she had just received from their father's top gunman. According to Freeze's father's partner, he had been kidnapped and brutally tortured. Strangely, no one knew where it came from or why it had happened. There was no ransom and he hadn't been robbed. No one tried to take over any of his spots, or territory. Nobody even bragged about it on the streets. It came and it went. After that, things took a drastic change for the worse.

Life as Freeze knew it began to rapidly fall apart as everybody who once professed to love his father and have his family's back stood back and watched. It seemed like every day his mother was selling a piece of jewelry, a car, or a property they once owned to keep food on the table, clothes on their backs, and a roof over their heads. Eventually they were forced to downsize from the extravagant home in the suburbs they were accustomed to, to a one-bedroom apartment in the hood. Ironically, they ended up in one of the same buildings that his father ran his operation out of. It was both the last resort and only choice. The transition wasn't easy at all. Now they had become exposed to the ghetto, overnight, with front-row seats. Freeze and his sister did their best to adjust quickly, but his mother struggled with coping with the sudden change. Freeze noticed the change in his mother's appearance after their relocation. Just like her fairy tale life she lived, her beauty queen features soon began to evaporate. Although his mother never experimented with drugs, she needed something to ease the pain she had endured in the recent months.

Now ten years old, after losing his father, life still seemed manageable for Freeze. Despite his resentment and hatred toward his father, Freeze realized he had inherited some of his father's strength. He dealt with the loss of his father by acting out in school. He bullied everyone he came in contact with, young or old, and dared anyone to challenge him back. One particular day Freeze got suspended from school for fighting. He was relieved that no one was answering the phone when the principal called his mother. That gave him extra time to edit his version of the incident before he got home. He planned to put on his usual innocent face and blame everything on everybody but himself. He knew his mother usually fell for his version.

As soon as Freeze got home, he felt a cold chill enter his body and then exit. He shook the feeling off as he entered the living room. He inhaled the fresh but strong scent of overused Pine-Sol, Lemon Ajax, and Comet mixed. He knew his mother had been on one of her cleaning binges again. He also knew she was always in a good mood whenever she cleaned up.

The tiny apartment was spotless, recalled Freeze. The pressure he had placed on his bladder since he had left school reminded Freeze that he had to use the bathroom. He grabbed hold of his crotch and made his way down the hall to where the bathroom was located. Freeze was already unbuckling his belt as he pushed the bathroom door open. He was so preoccupied with his pants that he didn't notice what was in front of him. His young eyes widened at the sight.

Freeze's first reaction was to scream from the shock. Instead, he just stood there in the bathroom doorway, forcing himself to be emotionless, to no avail. The sight of his mother foaming from the mouth, slumped on the toilet seat, opened up a floodgate of tears. He noticed a metal box sitting on her lap and dried-up blood resting at the bottom of her upper lip. Her eyes were still open, looking straight in his direction, but through him, matching the cold chill that he felt in the hallway.

Freeze didn't know what to do. He didn't know where to turn or how to digest what he was witnessing. He couldn't even process the hurt. So he stood tall, walked up closer to his mother, kissed her on her forehead, and looked down into the box. It contained a gun, drugs, and a wad of money. He removed the contents from the box and then backpedaled out of the bathroom. Freeze went back outside of the building and sat on the front steps until his sister's bus arrived. When it did, he shook his head at her, stopped her from entering the building, took her by the hand, and led her away. He went to the only place he knew he could go and be embraced with open arms.

Frenchie didn't know exactly what to do as his murdered best friend's kids showed up at his door with nowhere else to go. One thing was for sure to him: turning them away wasn't an option. Instead of a positive male role model for Freeze, he was like a ghetto tour guide. The streets became like a museum. Every scene had a story to be told and Frenchie seemed to know it all, from the beginning to the end. He taught Freeze everything he knew, mentally and intellectually preparing him. Freeze had no other choice but to end up in the streets.

He didn't know what happened to his mother after he left her body in the bathroom that day. He didn't even know if she had gotten a proper burial. Once again, life just went on. The police never even called the schools looking for her children. It was as if she was just one less person, deleted from existence. By the time Freeze was thirteen, once again the world that he had adapted and adjusted to took another drastic turn for the worse.

At 5:00 a.m., everything was calm and quiet. Five minutes after, the sound of a boom startled Freeze. Within seconds, the SWAT team units were in every room after knocking down the house door. Freeze was sound asleep with his father's pistol under his pillow. It made him feel safe, with a sense of power. He was protecting himself as well as his sister. So when he saw their room door being breached, out of instinct and still half asleep Freeze reacted. He retrieved the pistol and let off the remaining three rounds that were left in the barrel, barely missing the officers who nearly returned fire.

"Whoa! Whoa! It's a kid! It's a kid!" the leading officer yelled as he jumped in front of the other two SWAT team members' AR-15s with his hands up high.

Freeze dropped the smoking gun between his legs. It was as if he got high off of the gunpowder fumes he was inhaling. It gave him an instant rush. He sat in the bed, smiling. It was his first time actually discharging a gun. His aim was beyond terrible, but pulling the trigger was much easier than he thought.

Reality was brought back to him by his ten-year-old sister waking out of her sleep, screaming for her mother and father, while hugging her teddy bear tight. Two of the officers immediately rushed over and restrained Freeze. The leading officer confiscated the pistol.

They escorted Freeze outside of the room. The first thing he saw was Frenchie being cuffed up, still in his boxers. He had apparently put up a fight also. He was banged up pretty good, Freeze noticed. Frenchie looked over at young Freeze and cracked a smile of approval. He knew the sound of that familiar gun anywhere. Freeze smiled back and watched them take Frenchie away. Ultimately Freeze found out that he had been charged with two homicides and three kidnappings. It would be the last time he would see him for quite some time.

Being that Freeze nearly killed two officers, he was taken to a juvenile detention center. If it weren't for that, he would've been placed in foster care with his sister, who he lost contact with the entire time he was imprisoned.

Freeze had a rough time in the detention center. Most of the troubled teens there had lengthy sentences for serious crimes like murder and armed robbery. Many of the teens were huge compared to Freeze due to extensive workouts, and heavy eating. They had constantly picked on him and jumped on Freeze every chance they got. It seemed like every day he was being trapped in blind spaces from staff and was forced to defend himself. Freeze never backed down. He fought back and stood tall every time. Win or lose. He lost most of the time, but eventually he started getting his weight up just like his aggressors. Thereafter, Freeze stopped fighting fair. He kept two razors in his mouth at all times. Even in his sleep. He mastered the art of spitting, catching, and cutting, all in a single hand motion.

After a full year and a half, the Las Vegas, Nevada detention center was his to claim. Freeze put together a team of young convicts who were going home around the same time as him, and made plans to take over the streets the same way he did in the juvenile facility.

Freeze was released when he was seventeen years old. By the time he was eighteen, he was known as Freeze, a cold-hearted problem child.

He went back to claim the territory of his father's old buildings, and started from there. Using everything Frenchie had taught him, he was unstoppable. Their plans were to move everyone out of their way. Brute force was their favorite method of persuasion.

Freeze cruised down Las Vegas Boulevard in his CLS 550, smoking a blunt of haze and thinking. A lot had transpired in the past week. He needed to be away from everybody to clear his thoughts. He cracked his tinted driver's side window and plucked the ashes out into the warm midnight air as he made a left on Flamingo Road. He put the blunt back to his lips and took a deep pull, releasing the lung-cycled smoke from his nostrils. He zoned out to Kendrick Lamar as he pulled over to the side of the road, closed his eyes, laid his head back against the headrest, and reclined the electric seat all the way back, taking another hard hit of the drug that began sorting out his darkest thoughts.

The first thing he dwelled on was the incident that happened at Treasures the previous night. He realized that things could've gotten really ugly, had the head of the Double Gs not called him ordering him to defuse the situation immediately. *How the fuck did she find out about that shit so quick?* Freeze wondered. *That nigga Prime must be another one of them bitches' victims,* he concluded. But what really kept going through his mind was the woman in the red dress Prime was with. And how stupid it was for her to risk her life the way she did. It was the stupidest thing he had ever seen anyone do. That was the only truthful excuse he gave to his crew for backing down. There was no way he would have ever disclosed the entire reason and there was no way he could ever let any of them find out.

There was another major issue that stained Freeze's stimulated mind: Frenchie, and the reason the two had fallen out after being so close. The letter he had gotten from Frenchie two years into his bid haunted him for the entire second half of his time in the detention center. He regretted ever keeping in contact after he'd received it. Freeze felt betrayed.

It was a letter unlike any other that he received from him weekly. It revealed that all of Frenchie's appeals were denied, and him being sentenced to the death penalty was going to stick. According to the letter, he wanted to free his conscience of all mental burdens that had him trapped and make things right. He explained how he had known exactly what happened to Freeze's father and why. Most importantly, who did it. Freeze remembered shaking his head in disgust as he read how his father was killed by one of his young jealous female lovers. Although she had known about his wife and kids, she was enraged to find out that Freeze's father was expecting another baby by another young female from the housing projects across town. Freeze had never bothered to seek out his other sibling.

He had appreciated the clarity on his father's death, but he couldn't handle what Frenchie had written him about his mother. It was his heroin that his mother had overdosed on. He expressed how he felt he was responsible for his mother ODing on the drug. Freeze was crushed by the revelation. That day, he too placed blame on Frenchie. In his mind, he believed his mother would have still been alive had Frenchie not had the stash in the box. That letter marked the turning point of his bid and his life in general. That single letter, with nothing else to stand on, irreversibly transformed Anthony Frost into Freeze.

As if I don't have enough stuff on my plate. He felt as if he was somehow losing his grip on things in the streets, in his life. He knew before he could let that happen he had to do something.

With that being his only thought, Freeze took another hit of his blunt and pulled back into the ongoing traffic.

Chapter Nine

Monica woke up to the early morning sounds of birds chirping. The sun had just risen. The warm rays spread lightly across her beautiful naked body, which was tangled up in the linen sheets. A cool, refreshing breeze occasionally crept its way through the open balcony door, pampering her as she unintentionally overslept. She slowly opened her eyes and stared at the high, unfamiliar ceiling. She then sat up in a panic as reality hit her.

Oh my God! What did I do? I blew it! Oh shit! I blew it! Damn! She smacked her forehead with the palm of her hand and cursed herself.

She quickly scanned the lavish room for her clothes. They were across the room on the far end. She wrapped her body in the sheet and stood up. Her feet comfortably sank down into the plush carpet as she surveyed the room with surety that her mission was blown or at least compromised.

How much did I have to drink? she questioned herself as she felt her forehead while wobbling. She felt dizzy and could feel blood rushing to her brain. She looked around, trying to find anything that could salvage the mess that she had just gotten herself into. It would be all for nothing. *Nothing at all.*

Monica looked over at the balcony's glass door. It was wide open. She walked past it and went straight for her clothes. They were neatly folded, sitting on top of a plush leather loveseat that sat in front of a huge sixty-inch plasma flat screen hanging on the wall over a virtual fireplace, with *SportsCenter* playing on the screen.

As she tiptoed over and reached for her red dress, she noticed the pair of slacks folded right next to it. She looked behind her with caution to make sure she was still alone before feeling the pockets and digging in them. After finding what she was looking for, she opened up the gatorskin wallet and studied the driver's license. She looked at Prime's face, his name, and the address. She assumed that was where she was, instead of a hotel suite, due to of all the personal items in the room. She could even smell the odor of the ocean drifting through the open balcony door. She thoroughly searched through his cell phone contacts until she heard a noise. It sounded as if it came from within the room. She quickly put his stuff back the way she found it and began to get dressed. She had never realized that there was another door in the back of the room. It slowly opened.

Prime reemerged from the master bathroom with a huge smile on his face. He stood in the doorway with nothing on but a thick Polo towel wrapped around the lower half of his damp muscular body. He stared at Monica as she slithered her thickness back into her dress.

Monica turned and stared at him. She almost lost her breath as it all came back to her in minor glimpses and flashbacks. The restaurant, the food, the wine, the dancing, the ride back to his house, the walk on the beach, the flirting, the resistance, the temptation, the seduction, the sex, the regret, the blackout. It all seemed to be like a movie. And she wished it were.

She was sure that everything she had worked for was gone. The reality of losing it all began to introduce itself. She had waited for years for this opportunity. The position. The timing. The trust. The execution. She had the easy part compared to the rest of the operation. She couldn't fathom it all going to waste over something so meaningless.

Tears began to stream as she sat down on the edge of the sofa. She rested her elbows on her knees and her forehead into her hands. Her actions caught Prime totally off guard. His cocky smile turned into a look of warm compassion and concern. He rushed over and dropped to his knees directly in front of Monica. He was a sucker for a damsel in distress. Especially one he'd enjoyed as much as he had her. He put her head on his shoulder. She tried to push him away at first, but eventually embraced him as he begged her to let him know what was wrong.

Monica knew she couldn't reveal what really had her in tears and disturbed. *You jeopardized everything,* she beat herself up. She could feel Prime's eyes on her. She knew she had to tell him something. A thought quickly jumped in her head. "I'm so sorry. I'm stupid. You're going to kill me," she rambled.

"Whoa, slow up." Prime rubbed the side of her shoulders.

Monica lifted her head. When she did, she could see the genuine concern in Prime's eyes. At that moment she felt like shit. Despite his apparent occupation, Monica could see that he was a decent guy. Still, she had to remind herself of the bigger picture. Prime was just a small fish in a big pond. And small fish were often sacrificed for the bigger ones, Monica concluded. She took a deep breath before she continued. "I was only supposed to be using you. I'm so sorry," she blurted out.

Prime cocked his head back to look Monica in her eyes. Her words caught him by surprise. "Using me?" he repeated. He could already feel his temperature rising. He had felt that something was strange last night but she had put him at ease. He prided himself on being a man always on point and he couldn't believe he had almost gotten caught slipping.

"What?" he asked with a lot more aggression in his tone. He ended his physical support and now had her gripped by the side of the arms.

"Yeah. It's true. I was supposed to get close to you—" she confessed.

"For what? Like a . . . hit? You was put on me?" he jumped in before she could finish.

"Nooo!" She shook her head rapidly.

"But I supposed to be dead? You was setting me up for some niggas?" he boomed, already drawing his conclusion as to who had put Monica on him.

"No, I told you, and not exactly," she replied.

Prime scowled. "So, what the fuck is it?" he wanted to know. He was already searching around for his nearest pistol to help speed up the process.

Monica peeped it. "It's the Double Gs!" she exclaimed. "They wanted me to get close to you and tell you that Freeze was pillow talking about you so that it would cause tension or beef between the two of you," Monica confessed.

Prime's menacing look softened. His scowl was replaced with a smirk as he let out a light chuckle. "Did they choose me as a target? Or did you?" His demeanor was calm but stern.

"They did," she confirmed, still sobbing.

"I heard some shit about them bitches," he admitted. The name Double G had crossed his path on several occasions throughout the years. He had mainly heard it through the crooked cops and politicians he sometimes rubbed elbows with. At some point they all had asked him if he had any information on the organization, as if he had more clout and pull than the government or law enforcement. No one ever went into detail as to why they were inquiring, but somehow the Double Gs had tracked him down and he wanted to know more.

"Where are they? What do they want from me?" he asked all at once.

"I don't know. I don't know anything. I wouldn't have known until I got in. But now it's over. No one who had ever had sex with their intended target is allowed in."

"Well, how would they know?" he shot back. He had already begun to devise a plan.

"Trust me. They know almost everything else. This wouldn't be hard for them to find out," she proclaimed, lightening up on the tears while wiping her eyes. Prime's hands quickly joined hers with pure gentleness. Monica's eyes widened as she looked up with disbelief. *He should be smacking me up or trying to choke me to death by now.*

Prime was an opportunist and smart. He knew last night the sexy female in the red dress was too good to be true and he kept a watchful eye on her. He planned ahead like an expert chess player. He pretended not to see her texting someone while he was outside his car. His first thought was to drive off into the desert and leave her with a bullet in the back of her skull, but he instead decided to take full advantage of the situation. He thought Freeze had put her on to him, but he shook that notion off. That would be giving him too much credit, he knew. Now he was getting closer to the truth. He put his softest tone on as he forced her head right back onto his shoulder.

"It's okay. Don't cry. I'll get you in. Just tell me what it is that I have to do," he stated, trying to conceal the tone of his hidden intentions in his voice. Everything had unfolded right on schedule. The drug he had slipped into her drink last night actually sped things up. There was much more time to play now, but at the end of the day, for Prime, it was all about business.

Behind Prime's back, Monica had a hidden smile of her own. Twisting the truth was her last resort and it worked perfectly. She couldn't believe that Prime had bought her story. True, she had been put on him by the Double Gs, but the instructions she was given were not what she had just told Prime. He had no clue or idea about her intended plan that he nearly foiled, who she really was, or what she was really going after. *I guess drug dealers really aren't as smart as they think they are,* she concluded, pulling the wool over Prime's eyes so easily.

Ten minutes later, Prime was fake strapped to his bed and was reading the memo that the Double Gs required their victims to read on the handheld recorder Monica possessed.

If he only knew what they really had new recruits do to their potential victims, he would've definitely tried to kill me, she thought.

Chapter Ten

Rob-C spent the last fifteen minutes yelling into his cell phone at the top of his lungs. He paced back and forth across his living room's hardwood floors inhaling a mouthful of the loud-smelling blunt in between each line of the escalated dialogue.

"I don't give a fuck, bitch! It's whatever. I ain't one of those fuckin' puppets connected to your strings. You got the wrong nigga! You got me fucked up! I'm R-o-b to the mother fuckin' C! This conversation is over. Lose my fuckin' numba!" he yelled into his iPhone.

He partially heard the woman on the other end try to calmly respond before he hung up on her in midsentence.

Feeling the extra boost of confidence, he relit the blunt as it went out and then he went into the bathroom for the second half of his ritual. He pulled down his pants and backed his 280-pound ass onto the porcelain toilet seat. A few seconds later, his phone rang again; he checked the caller ID and declined the call, returning to his thoughts.

He looked at the time on his Rolex watch and calculated a quick estimation. He had almost a half hour to drop off a brick and a half of coke to one of his workers. Rob-C controlled the entire east side of North Las Vegas. Every hustler up there either had his work or was at least supposed to. And he planned to keep it that way. He paid his goons well. He figured that after he got off of the toilet, there would be just enough time for him to get to his stash house and over to the drop-off location on schedule. He believed in clockwork and punctuality when it came to any type of business legal or illegal.

Rob-C thumbed through a *Straight Stuntin'* magazine. He stopped in his tracks when he heard a sudden knock on the door. It startled him for a second. He wasn't expecting any company. He was super cautious. No one knew where he lived. Not even his main girl. He quickly wiped his ass, hiked up his pants up in nervous haste, and exited the bathroom. He snatched up his Glock from the dresser and made his way into the living room, tiptoeing in case he wanted to act like nobody was home. He was still very anxious to peek out the curtains to see who it could be. Just as he got close, he flinched as a flashlight beam hit him. Two flashlight beams swayed back and forth, followed by a hard tap on the window. Shadows of faces appeared out of nowhere and Rob-C was faced with a drug dealer's worst nightmare.

"Open up! It's the police!"

Rob-C didn't know what to do. He was sure they had seen him. He made a quick mental assessment. The house was clean aside from a few jars of weed in his coat pocket. He also had a registered gun with all of the necessary documents in his bedroom closet. He felt he was straight. If he was wanted for any of his illegal activities, they would be so big that he was sure it would be the Feds kicking in his door with SWAT, not local police announcing themselves with flashlights.

Rob-C quickly got himself together. He sniffed his own shirt, noticing the fact that it and the entire living room smelled like purple haze. He nonchalantly brushed it off and opened the door with the safety chain still on.

"Can I help you?" he asked the black officer.

The white officer stepped up, shining the light into Rob-C's face and inside of the house while he spoke. "We received a call about a loud domestic dispute. It was reported to this address. Is there anyone else here with you?"

Rob-C was confused at first. And then he thought about the out-of-control phone conversation he had just had and he laughed to himself, but still he wondered how his neighbors had heard him. He figured that they had to be eavesdropping in the first place. So he brushed it off, expecting the cops to go away.

"Nah. Nobody's here with me. I'm alone. Everything's cool. The neighbors probably just heard me on the horn," Rob-C explained through the cracked door.

The white cop acted as if he didn't quite buy the story. He looked past Rob-C and never stopped shining the light into the house the whole time they stood there. "Well, I hope you can understand that since the O.J. incident, we just need to be sure," he seriously joked, to lighten the mood. "So if you don't mind, we'd just like to have a quick look around and we'll be on our way."

Rob-C instantly got defensive. He was tempted to ask for a warrant, but thought better of it. He knew his crib was clean, so there was no reason to draw extra attention to himself than he was already doing just by having the cops on his porch. He realized they weren't leaving, so he felt it was better to let them in so the nosey passers-by could at least wonder which house they were at as opposed to having the answer right in front of them.

"Okay. Look. I was really on my way out. So please, just make this quick," Rob-C asked them as he closed the door, unchained it, and reopened it.

"Go 'head, Blake. I'll be in the car," the black cop stated.

"Ten-four, Douglass," Officer Blake confirmed.

Rob-C shut the door behind them. He led the officer upstairs first in an attempt to distract him from the weed scent, giving the downstairs more time to air out. It was no use though. Rob-C turned to the officer as he reached the top of his steps. He was sure by the look on Officer Blake's face that he had smelled the strong aroma. There was no way of knowing why the broad smile appeared across the officer's face though. Rob-C had no clue as to why the officer was so adamant about entering his home or why he was really there.

Ten minutes later, Officer Blake returned to the passenger side of the squad car. Office Douglass just stared at him, watching as he sat down and closed the door, removing his standard-issue leather gloves.

"Well?" Officer Douglass uttered.

Officer Blake glanced over at his partner. Instead of responding, he reached for the charcoal gray unmarked car's radio and cleared his throat. He instantly got into character. "We have a black male, five foot nine, late thirties, down! He appears to have been strangled. No signs of a breach or a perp. I need medical assistance and forensics notified," Officer Blake radioed in.

Officer Douglass dropped his head in shame as he sat in the driver's seat across from his partner. He had taken an oath to protect and serve but for the past few years of the seven years he had been on the force he had been dishonoring that oath.

"This just ain't right," he shook his head and uttered under his breath as he pulled out his small flip phone Blake had been given when the blackmailing began. Although years had gone by, he was still trying to figure out how he had allowed himself to get tangled up in the web he found himself stuck in.

"Come on partner, not today." Blake grimaced. "This was the last one, buddy," he offered, before Douglass had the chance to complain about their conduct for the past three-plus years. He too knew what they were, or rather he was, doing was wrong, but he had no choice or say-so in the matter. He had made his bed and knew he had to lie in it. The video he had been forced to watch was still burned in the back of his mind. His fetish for young hookers had cost him more than money could ever buy. It had been a hard pill for him to swallow, but he had been living with being the Double Gs' puppet. What ate at him the most was the fact that he had dragged his partner, who he knew was as clean as an old wooden squeaky screen door up until this, into his mess and corrupted him, tarnishing his reputation. That was his biggest regret, but he was grateful to have a friend like him.

"I promise," Blake reassured him.

Douglass looked over at him. "I hope so, bro." Both his stare and words were solid.

Blake faced him. "We're on the same page. The sooner you let them know, the sooner this'll all be over and we can go back to being the good cops we've always been prior to my hiccup," he replied.

Douglass nodded. He opened the flip. Target deleted, he texted to the woman he knew as Starr: the mastermind behind the predicament Blake had gotten him.

A thumbs-up emoji followed by a smiley face was the reply he received.

"This fucking bitch!" he cursed at her arrogance. "This really better be it, Blake!"

"What now?" Blake scowled.

Douglass showed him the screen of his phone. Blake chuckled.

"Shit ain't funny!" Douglass bellowed. "You lucky I fucking love you, bro," he reminded Blake.

The two formed an unbreakable bond the moment they became partners six years ago. They had been having one another's back both personally and professionally from day one. Which was why Douglass had even considered hearing his partner out. Had it not been for the story his partner had told him, which had been forcing him to break the law, Douglass knew he would have never agreed to aid his partner in murder or any other crimes for that matter. Although he was empathetic to what had happened to Blake and this was not their first time doing something illegal, it was still bothering him that his partner had just committed murder and made him an accessory. Officer Douglass was glad to hear that this would be their last and final time doing something that went against their shield, because he didn't know how much more or if for any longer he could take it.

For your sake, partner, this better be over, was Officer Douglass's last thought before he exited the car with the yellow crime scene tape.

Chapter Eleven

Normally, on a late Monday night, Club Panties would be completely closed. For the most part, it was. Starr, Diamond, Bubbles, and Felicia were at the round table. Starr sat in the huge leather desk chair, on the phone with Queen Fem, while the other three girls stood in front of the glass oval-shaped cherry wood–grained table counting hundreds of thousands of dollars that was about to be moved from the club to the safe house. They could tell the conversation wasn't going too well. At times, it seemed as if Starr and Queen Fem never got along. They barely ever saw eye to eye. It was an apparent power struggle that quietly seemed to be getting out of control.

Queen Fem and Starr had two different visions for the Double Gs. While Queen Fem had been off the grid while flying under the radar for over a decade, Starr had been right there on the front-line, running the Double G organization with an iron fist and becoming a force to be reckoned with to those who would go against them or rebel against her demand. She felt that she had every right to make major decisions on her own without consulting her. That was second to the fact that she turned a vengeful motorcycle gang into a half-billion dollar empire. Queen Fem's problem with her young successor was that she had allowed the Double Gs to become too exposed. She had designed the organization in a way in which whenever a target was chosen and a move was being executed they were to not be seen and barely ever heard. She had expressed to Starr on many occasions how she had felt where she meant for them to be ghosts that haunted, Starr transformed them into wolves that hunted.

Both women's methods were effective so neither of them ever backed down, or away. Both women's patience was running thin with the other's method. The battle of old school versus new school was evident to those privy to the conversation. The others were counting up the last few stacks of money and packing them into the duffel bag. They couldn't help but overhear every single word that Starr freely screamed into the air as they went back and forth. It was obvious to the other members of the Double Gs that their boss and founder were unable to reach an agreement.

"Listen, Starr. You're still not comprehending the reality of this organization," Queen Fem continued. "Power is never for sale. It is gained, earned, and exercised until the person or people in control lose it. You don't sell it or give it away. And definitely not back to the source that it came from. So I'm rejecting your ideas in every form. Please, don't go against me on this. There will only be consequences. Severe. We cannot jeopardize what we have. Definitely not for money. No matter the amount. So stick to the script and play by the rules. This conversation is over and will not be brought up again."

The phone went dead in Starr's ear. She looked at the receiver with disbelief before violently slamming it back down into the cradle. She felt she had just been indirectly threatened and she didn't like it one bit. The Double Gs had become hers to claim, although Queen Fem still had many followers from the original group who stayed with her and protected her. But Starr and her movement was the new school. The future. The only problem was that Queen Fem possessed all of the G-Files, which Starr needed to execute her future vision for the organization.

Starr was trying to convince Queen Fem that instead of just stacking up the G-Files without putting them to use, they should sell them back to certain victims, which would generate millions in the high hundreds over a short period of six months. Queen Fem never even entertained the idea. Once a victim was in the G-Files, he was stuck for life. It wasn't about money. It was about position and power for her. One was never far behind the other. Aside from that, how Queen Fem had come to be both in possession and control of the G-Files was more valuable than the organization itself. It was also the reason she was one of the most dangerous women on the West Coast, not to mention one of the most wanted.

Still, one thing Queen Fem stated early in the conversation stood out to Starr: "You're trying to show me a way to make more money. I'm proving a way to enhance more power that money can't buy. In the end, money is paper. Go to Cuba with all of the money in the world, they'll kill you. Why? Because they have more power. Your money is useless. But if you overtake your island with power, you control everyone that comes in with money."

Queen Fem's words went right over Starr's head. All she could think about was the secret that she had on her mentor and how damaging it could be if it ever got out. Starr hoped it never got to that point where she felt her hand was forced.

Chapter Twelve

Special Agent McCarthy stayed in the federal building all night waiting for the call he was banking on. He glanced at his watch. It was nearly half an hour past the time he was expecting the incoming call. Under any normal circumstances it wouldn't have been an issue, but in this particular situation he knew thirty minutes late could possibly mean you were dead. He shook the thought out of his head. He didn't want to speak or think anything wrong or bad into existence. Besides, he really needed to ring with something he could go off of. Every informative phone call brought him closer to taking down the Double Gs, he felt. He seemed to be the only one taking the operation seriously. Had he not been so high ranking, he was sure none of the leads he received would have been followed up on. He knew no one really took the case seriously. It was the joke of the Bureau, but not to Agent McCarthy. He knew exactly what the Double Gs were capable of. He answered the phone on the first ring.

"Sheep here," he chimed into the office phone.

"This is wolf in sheep's clothing," the woman stated, using the code words confirming her identity and the fact that she wasn't in distress.

"Tell me something good," he replied in a tone as low as hers.

"Well, I'm kinda stagnant. It's real hard to get any closer now. I'm trying to work my way up, but there are so many people in the way. We have a meeting next month. I'm going to finally bring a mic in to record what's going on. Right now, that's the best I can do. But I do have this one thing. I think they had this drug dealer who called himself Rob-C murdered. And I think they used the police to do it."

Agent McCarthy's eyebrows rose. "What? What makes you say that?"

"I can't get into it right now, but I overheard it while I was in the club. Some people were laughing about what happened at his funeral."

"What happened?"

"A video that was supposed to be a documentary of his life was passed out to everyone who attended. But instead, it was footage of him getting sodomized and all sorts of degrading stuff. Apparently, he was under the impression that he had bought his way out of the blackmail by paying $500,000 to Starr. But it wasn't the original copy."

"So why do you think the police killed him?"

"They were ordered to. The guy must've refused to do something. Someone's coming. I have to go. But look into it yourself. I'll text you and let you know the next time we can speak."

"Okay. Good work. Just push hard to get in position. I'm giving you the full green light. Do whatever you have to. I got you covered. Do whatever it takes to get to Queen Fem. Find out exactly who she is and where she's at!"

McCarthy cursed at the sound of the dial tone. He wasn't sure how much his plant had heard, but he hoped she'd heard enough to get the picture.

Chapter Thirteen

Starr navigated her black Maserati Quattro sport with the cruise control set exactly on sixty-five, which was the speed limit. It was the middle of the night and there seemed to be only a handful of cars on Interstate 15 South. She was usually a speed demon, but tonight she had to be extra cautious. She had in her trunk the duffel bags full of money that was just counted up. She didn't want any complications. She was only mere miles away before she reached her exit to the safe house just outside of Las Vegas. She had been driving for nearly an hour and a half to the California residence. Between the quiet, dark highway and the fact that she was somewhat tired, it had seemed longer to her. The music was nearly on full blast and both the driver's side and passenger's side windows were evenly cracked, leveling the crisp breeze, just to keep her awake and alert. Every few seconds she made sure her eyes rotated past her rearview and side mirrors.

Her concentration was broken by the sound of her cell phone's ringtone blaring out of her car's dashboard speakers. The screen read Private. She became irritated like she always did.

"Hello!" she snapped.

"I know I said the next one would cost you, but I've decided to give you another free courtesy call, to prove a point," the voice announced.

Starr immediately recognized the familiar anonymous caller's voice from the first call she had received before. "What point is that?" Starr wanted to know. She was pissed to the max that somebody was able to play games with her and be a step ahead of her when she was used to being in control.

"That this is real. I'm real and this is not a game," the caller replied.

"Nah, you definitely playing games, muthafucka," Starr barked.

The caller chuckled. "I should hang up on your disrespectful ass, but I'ma let that slide. Since you think I'm playing games, look behind you." The caller paused.

His words were enough to put Starr on full alert. She shook her head and stretched her eyes. She reached for her dashboard and pressed a button. Within seconds, every image behind her vehicle appeared on the small four-inch screen.

She had activated the rearview camera monitor's night vision. Starr squinted and focused on the monitor. She noticed a set of distinct headlights she had noticed nearly an hour ago trailing a short distance behind her. She thought nothing of it the first time, but now the anonymous caller confirmed what she had once thought. She had tailed enough people to recognize when she was being tailed herself.

"How do I know that's not you following me?"

"You don't," he answered calmly.

Starr watched carefully. She noticed how all the other cars switched lanes, sped up, and maneuvered around the trucks. But the black Chevy Caprice maintained its speed and lane. It was a textbook tail, she thought. Starr wondered, if it wasn't the caller then who could it be? She knew there were only three options: the law enforcement for the Double Gs, stick up kids for the money in the trunk, or a hit. The more she tossed around the thought the more an attempt on her life stood out. *Queen.*

"Thanks," Starr retorted and then abruptly disconnected the call with the anonymous caller. It felt good to hang up on the caller, thought Starr. She was sure her move caught the caller off guard and that's exactly what she wanted. She touched a button on her screen to activate her car phone's voice command. "Queen Fem," she stated clearly into the air. She could instantly hear the digital sequence tone dialing by the sophisticated computer system.

"Here," Queen Fem answered in a flat tone.

Starr got straight to the point. "I'm being tailed. Is it on your call?"

Queen Fem let out a devilish snicker. "Please, darling. Hardly. You wouldn't see it coming and you know that. Besides, even though we barely see eye to eye these days, I do need you. Anyway, what's the problem?"

"A black Caprice. Dark tints. They've been on me for quite some time."

"Feds, maybe?"

"I don't know, might be. I can't tell. Even if it is, they'll try to take the money I'm transporting to the safe house."

"Well, you have to lose them. But if it isn't them, that makes our problem even worse, but solvable."

"What do you suggest?"

"Well, you obviously can't lead them to the safe house. Stay on the highway. Keep going straight for as long as you can. They have no idea of where you're going, so they won't know they've been made and their cover's been blown."

"What are you gonna do?"

"You mean, what are we gonna do?" Queen Fem corrected her. "This is where part of my previous point during our earlier conversation comes into play."

"Now is not the time, Queen," Starr retorted.

"Okay, look, keep them on you. Wait for my signal. We'll trap them off. You take care of the rest."

"How will I know your signal?" Starr asked, confused.

"Trust me. I believe that we have much more power than you think."

"If that's the case why don't we just call your inside contacts and find out if it is the Feds? We can deal with anyone else."

Queen Fem sighed with frustration at the fact that her protégé just didn't get it. "Because, we always have to seem to be in control. And we are. There is no one above us. That's the message we send. So no matter who is in that vehicle, it must be clear that we are not to be taken lightly. Whoever sent them will find that out shortly. Good-bye, Starr. We'll speak shortly. I'm going back to bed. Watch for the signal. You can fill me in on the details later."

The car went silent again. Starr had no idea what Queen Fem's signal would be. She was rarely ever specific about anything. Just then

Starr's phone rang. She shook her head at the caller ID.

"You're a rude chick, you know that." It was more of a statement than a question.

Rather than reply, Starr rolled her eyes.

"I told you before, the first one, and now the second, was free. Nothing else is free."

Starr noticed a change in the caller's tone.

"If you want to know who, what, when, and how, the price is two million in cash, nonnegotiable. I'll be in touch." The call went dead.

Starr slammed her hand down forcefully on her dashboard. She couldn't believe someone was trying to blackmail and bully her, a man at that. There was no way she was having that, especially when that was her forte. Starr made a mental note to investigate both the calls and the allegations. Right now she had other important matters to address. Rather than wait around for Queen Fem's signal, she activated her car phone's voice command to place another call.

Chapter Fourteen

"So, how does it feel?" Felicia asked Monica. She let out a gust of smoke from the Cuban she was puffing on, as they posted up in front of the Bellagio, watching the water show on the Las Vegas strip.

Monica peered over at her. "How does what feel?" A clueless look appeared across her face.

It was Felicia's turn to cut her eyes over at Monica. She took another short pull of the cigar. "To be the president, bitch!" she chimed. "What you think? You a Double G now!" she followed up with.

Monica let out a light chuckle. Up until the moment Felicia had mentioned it, she hadn't given it any real thought. Her mind had been elsewhere. She couldn't shake the close call she had with Prime. The position she had put herself in along with the measures she had to go to in order to do damage control had her on edge. She was still beating herself up over it. The thought of jeopardizing everything she had worked so hard to become had her feeling uneasy. On top of it all, she was well aware of the fact that if either party found out the truth about the other's intent, she was as good as dead. She could feel Felicia's eyes on the side of her face.

"My bad, girl, I'm tripping." A huge smile accompanied her words.

"You's a silly bitch." Felicia shook her head. "Just don't get silly when it comes time to handle business, because this no joke." Her words came out sharp. She stared Monica square in the eyes as she spoke, never blinking. "One silly-ass move could cost not only you, but all of us, understand me?"

Monica nodded. Felicia's words jolted through her entire body as she spoke in the authoritative tone. She could see why she was higher up in the rankings of the organization she had just recently joined. From day one, since the two had met and conversed at the club, Felicia had always spoken to her in a serious and militant type of manner. If one didn't know any better, you would have thought that she had been in the military. Familiar with it herself, Monica noticed how Felicia's demeanor resembled that of a drill sergeant. But Monica believed that to not be the case. Although she had never asked nor was it volunteered to her, she was sure Felicia came from a rough background. She was sure if it ever came down to it, Felicia would be one of the main ones to watch out for.

The blaring sound of classical music illuminated as water shot into the air. The applause by tourists and locals drew Monica and Felicia's attention to the entertainment behind them. Despite them both being Las Vegas bred and seeing the water show countless times, it was always a beautiful sight for them to see. As water continued to springboard from out of the main body of water, matching the rhythm of the music, people clapped, cheered, recorded, and took pictures. The show put Felicia and Monica in a chill mode. Monica leaned over the light gray stone railing and rested her elbows on it, while Felicia hopped up on it. She relit her cigar and took a long drag.

"If only life could be this peaceful er'day," she cooed as she filled the air with a mist of cigar smoke.

"Wishful thinking," Monica retorted.

Felicia chuckled. "Bitches like us don't get the 'happily ever after' stories."

Just then, reality set in. Felicia looked down and retrieved her vibrating iPhone 6 Plus from her hip. Unlocking her phone, she immediately went to the incoming text message from Starr. Her eyes did a quick scan of the message.

"We gotta go!" Felicia hopped down from the railing.

"Is everything okay?" Monica could see the change in her demeanor all over her face.

"Yeah, it will be," Felicia answered as she looked left then right at the ongoing traffic on both sides of the four lanes. "Starr needs us," she added as she darted into the street.

Chapter Fifteen

Federal Agents Mullin and Craven had been tailing Starrshma Fields since she had left Club Panties. Agent Mullin, who was the driver, tried his best to stay undetected, but there wasn't enough cover traffic on the highway to blend in with. At times, it would get frustrating because all the trucks would unavoidably obstruct their view, which was a constant threat of them missing whatever exit Starr would get off.

So far, they felt they had kept a comfortable cushion. It was a fairly easy assignment given directly by Head Special Agent McCarthy. The orders were unmistakable. "Stay on her. Don't let her out of your sight." Agent Mullin filled up on coffee while Agent Craven tossed back a six pack of Red Bulls like they were Heinekens.

"Where the hell's she goin'?" Agent Craven rhetorically asked Agent Mullin as he flapped his legs open and closed, feeling as if his bladder would soon burst.

"Who knows? That's the whole point of tracking her. It's our job to find out," Agent Mullin condescendingly retorted.

Agent Craven let the little smart remark slide. "Damn. Well I hope she pulls over at a rest stop soon. What? Broads don't piss?"

"She probably was smarter than you and tinkled before she left." Agent Mullin chuckled. "Wish ya still had the empty cans now, huh?"

"I'd much rather use your coffee mug. Now shut up and drive!" Agent Craven finally snapped with attitude.

Agent Mullin chuckled. The two weren't partners. They just were paired up by Agent McCarthy because they were both the newest rookies. Agent McCarthy figured there wouldn't be any real excitement or danger to the task, so none of his wild cowboys would've jumped for babysitting a woman. None of them were taking the case seriously yet. Somehow, they felt they needed more proof. So far, in their eyes, the phantom vigilante bicycle Girl Scouts gang, as they nicknamed them, were doing them all a favor. Criminals were finally feeding off criminals.

Agent Mullin was twenty-six years old. He still looked every bit of eighteen. He was a scrawny, red-haired, white kid with a pencil neck who wore a weird-looking pair of glasses. He tried to wear suits to make his appearance demand more respect. Nobody in the Bureau bought it. He was a kid, a rookie. His hands were too clean. Around the Bureau, you were respected by triumphing over cases and high-profile job details. That was how one agent was introduced to another.

"Hey! What could be worse than a stalkin' chick who doesn't like dick, huh? At least mosta the ones I tailed I had a real shot at bangin'. You know, as a service for the Bureau. The things I do for my country!" one of the agents clowned in his natural Italian accent. *Laughter erupted heavily and then the room got quiet as the agent seemed to get serious for a second, pointing at them as he spoke.*

"Hey, you guys, watch ya asses out there." And then he snickered. *"No, for real. Watch your asses out there. I hear them broads is inta some pretty kinky stuff. There are things they like to do to you with your nightstick, if you know what I mean, eh?"*

The rest of the agents applauded the ignorance and blew loud whistles by sticking their fingers into their mouths as they watched the two rookies mope into Agent McCarthy's office.

"Cops have nightsticks. Feds have paper badges," Agent Mullin whispered to Agent

Craven as if the joke was really on all of the other agents. Agent Craven hated Agent Mullin from that day forward.

Agent Craven was a twenty-seven-year-old black guy already ahead of his time. He had married his high school sweetheart right after they graduated. He got her pregnant shortly after. She stayed home while he went off to college and then entered the academy. He claimed it was all for a setup to be able to take care of his responsibilities, but really it was his way of escaping them with legit reasons. He felt he needed more excitement.

Agent Mullin banged down on the steering wheel as one of the large eighteen-wheeler Ford trucks cut in front of him, blocking his view of Starr.

"Damn it! I really wish I could just cut on the siren," he complained.

"That would be real subtle, jackass. And it would also defeat the purpose," Agent Craven sarcastically snapped.

"Whatever. I'm going around him," Agent Mullin replied. He cut the steering wheel to the left in an attempt to get over in the passing lane. Out from behind him, another furniture truck sped by and crossed in front of the Chevy, sealing off the passing lane.

"Just great!" Agent Mullin sarcastically yelled out as he sucked his teeth. The two trucks rode side by side in front of them. He had lost view of Starr's Maserati, but he knew she was still up ahead because they weren't near any upcoming exits.

A third truck pulled from deep behind and cut on the right side of the unmarked vehicle. It sealed off the shoulder lane. Now, all three trucks cruised together at the same speed, forming a moving wall. None of them had rear license plates.

"What the fuck?" Agent Craven rhetorically gasped as he rose up in his seat.

Before they knew it, two more trucks came from behind them. They split up on each side, one on the left, one on the right. Now the agents couldn't see in front of them or on either side.

"It's a trap! It's a fuckin' trap!" Agent Craven yelled.

"No shit, Sherlock!" Agent Mullin retorted. "Radio it in. Hurry!" Agent Mullin tried to maneuver, but there was nothing he could do. Just as he was about to slam down on the brakes and abort, three more trucks accelerated to seal off every lane behind them, boxing them in while shining their bright high beams directly into the back of the car, blinding them as the reflection bounced off the back doors of the trucks in front, back into the car. They could barely see.

Agent Craven fumbled the radio and dropped it on the floor by accident. He bent down to pick it up. Two loud, roaring sounds came from behind them. The trucks slightly separated opening up a slim gap of space. Two motorcycles with passengers slipped through the crack and approached the Chevy. One was on the right, another was on the left. Long hair was flying from under the four helmets. The two passengers on the back were pointing pistols at the windows of Agents Mullin and Craven. Neither agent noticed the sudden presence of the machines. The girls tried hard to see through the tint with the help of the trucks' high beams shining light through the back, but all they made out was shadows. That was all they needed.

Agent Craven found a firm grip on the radio and put it to his mouth while he was still on the floor. He looked up at Agent Mullin's shining face and then something drew his attention to the window. He released the radio and went for his Sig, but it was too late. Glass from the unmarked car shattered as nine millimeter slugs invaded the window of the vehicle and caused it to spin out of control. The left side of Agent

Mullin's face was ripped open and sprayed blood all over Agent Craven. A separate clip was emptied into the back of Agent Craven's own skull while he was still hunched over on the floor. The trucks quickly broke up and the two motorcycles initiated their brakes as the Chevy fishtailed and crashed into a guardrail. It flipped over three full times after the last truck nicked the bumper as it passed by. The trucks honked their horns and then vanished into the night.

Starr still drove on cruise control. Although she couldn't see, she had an idea what was going on behind her. When it was all over, the two riders who occupied the motorcycles lifted their front wheels up high into the air then let them down, picked up speed, and zoomed past her. That was the all the confirmation she needed to know everything had gone according to plan.

With her problem solved, Starr veered off to the upcoming exit. Once off, she drove to the nearest gas station to the right of her, where she texted Felicia and told her where she'd be once the heat was off of her back. She pulled into the lot, parked on the side of the restroom area, and left the keys in the ignition with the engine running. She removed the rest of her sole possessions, wiped it down, and deleted the car phone's memory chip. She threw everything into one of the duffel bags full of money and awaited her new ride.

Twenty minutes later, two black Ducatis pulled up and on the side of her. The riders were dressed in all black leather, from head to toe. Starr walked up to the one closest to her and took the rider's helmet as she dismounted the bike. She strapped both of the duffle bags to the back of the bike and then climbed on. The driver of the bike jumped in the Maserati and backed up. Starr and the other motorcyclist did the same. Within seconds they all headed in different directions.

Chapter Sixteen

Agent McCarthy's house phone echoed through the darkness of his bedroom, while he lay face flat into his pillow. Irritated from his rest being broken, he extended his left forearm out from under the comforter and retrieved the phone. He grunted into the receiver as a greeting. The caller's words on the other end suddenly had him wide awake.

"What?" he yelled as he spun over on to his back and sat upright. He had managed to tangle himself up in the bed sheets and expose his wife's nakedness in the process. The sudden coolness from the air conditioned, chilled room woke Linda McCarthy. She moaned and mumbled something inaudible as she reached for the covers to no avail. When the bright light from the nightstand's lamp lit up their bedroom, she slowly rolled over to see what all the commotion was about.

"What's wrong, dear?" she asked in the softest tone.

He turned to peck her on the lips as he stuck his legs into his boxers and pants at the same time. "Nothing, honey. Go back to sleep. I have to go out into the field for a few hours."

Linda knew it was something serious, but knew he just didn't want to alarm her. She knew she would get the details later anyway from her job, the newspaper headlines, or both. She lay back down, repossessed the sheets, rewrapped her naked body, and rolled back over in his spot. She watched him bounce around the room in haste before finally cutting the light back out and kissing her good-bye at the same time. She knew that specific kiss all too well. It was the one he used after being reminded that any day could be his last.

Agent McCarthy floored the gas pedal of his Audi A8 as he ripped through the highway like it was an Indy 500 racetrack. Traffic was clear for most of the way. There was still a heavy flow of semi trucks, but they moved out of the way and warned each other over their CB radios at the sound of the siren's flashing lights that was magnetized to the Audi's rooftop. He felt as if it was all his fault. He forced himself to believe that the blood was on his hands and nobody else's. It was his operation. His call. And he sent two young rookies up against the most professional criminal enterprise structure that he had ever seen or ever heard of. Anger rose within him as his dipped in and out of the lanes, trying to picture how it all happened. Other than the shells, the tire marks, and the area of the murder scene, he was informed that not many clues were left.

The Audi slowed down at the sight of swirling lights up ahead. He pulled over alongside of the dented guardrail, as close to the wrecked Chevy as he could, and jumped out, leaving his door wide open. As he strongly walked toward the scene, he noticed that the immediate area was taped off. The sight was far from pretty; there were countless numbered yellow markers scattered, labeling the shell casings. The air still smelled of stale gunpowder, burnt rubber, engine oil, gasoline, blood, and most of all death. Agent McCarthy walked up to the vehicle and could tell all eyes were on him. The CSIs of the violent crimes unit stopped what they were doing as the other agents spoke in a lower tone than before.

"You see these?" Agent Mullin's bloody head rested on the steering wheel. The entire left side of his face had been eaten up by each bullet that struck him at such a close proximity. Even his shattered teeth were exposed through his skinless jaw. His eyes were still open, staring through the portal of life. Sadly, they were facing the exit. His seat belt was still on. Broken glass was everywhere Agent McCarthy could see. He slowly stuck his head farther into the vehicle and looked back.

He noticed Agent Craven had been thrown into the back seat of the car. Blood leaked from the back of his head and neck. His vest, which he wore on the outside of his shirt, was riddled with bullets. Agent McCarthy also noticed the soiling around Agent Craven's crotch. As he looked closer he noticed something else. He called out for a member of the CSI unit to come over and use a gloved hand to pick up and pull out the strange object. The CSI officer looked at it oddly and then dropped it into a small clear plastic evidence bag before handing it over to Agent McCarthy. It was a blue hard plastic tile with an engraved circular human stick figure with a tri-angle dress at the waist. Agent McCarthy knew exactly what it was. It was a gender sign peeled off the door of a woman's public restroom. It was a message to the Federal Bureau of Investigation. The Double Gs apparently wanted them to know they were responsible.

It infuriated Agent McCarthy. "Let's go, people!" he turned around and shouted. He looked over at the CSI. "You, dust this for fingerprints. Tag and bag whatever evidence you can find. I want to know exactly what happened like I was in this vehicle myself. Speaking of which, get me that fuckin' tape! ASAP! And I want an APB on the car they were tracking! Now!"

After leaving the scene, Agent McCarthy headed back to the Bureau. He got off of the elevator and went straight to his office. He shut the door behind him, further enclosing the silence of the already lifeless building. It all started to weigh down on him heavily. He removed his suit jacket and tie, and then folded them over the back of his desk chair before strolling over to his file cabinet. He reluctantly unlocked it and removed the folders of both deceased agents. He let them fall flat on his desk as he sat down and just stared down at them. Minutes passed before he was able to bring himself to open them up.

He then reviewed their entire careers and their personal lives. It was all there. Everything was written out on paper. And, now that's all they would be: statistics, he thought. He knew if something wasn't done, the files would be red stamped DECEASED or TERMINATED and would be stored away, probably never to be seen again.

It wasn't like Agent McCarthy hadn't experienced death on his watch or under his command before. That wasn't the issue that ate at him inside. It was the fact that a wrong call he made resulted in two men losing their lives. Agent McCarthy banged his fist on his desk. One thing became absolutely clear to him: there wouldn't be any more slipups or underestimations of any sort anymore from here on out.

Chapter Seventeen

She had been driving the Maserati Quattro Sport on the back roads for over an hour. She was almost at the specified location she was given. A few minutes later, she approached it slowly, with extreme caution. This was the biggest assignment given to her by the Double Gs since she had become a member, one that would earn trust and get her further ahead and deeper inside. She pulled into the long, dark sandlot. It was a construction site. The office building was far in the back. She parked behind it and pulled out her cell phone. She dialed another number that was already programmed in the untraceable phone strictly for Double G business affairs. It rang and a woman answered.

"I'm here," she declared. Once that was established, she disconnected the call, then pulled out her own cell phone and punched in a different number. It too was untraceable. A male voice answered.

"It's me," she announced herself and began reporting details about what had happened. She explained what she knew and heard all the way up to the time she switched her bike for Starr's car.

"Look, this shit is getting too deep. I got it from here," he proclaimed.

"It's too late. I'm already on. I intend to finish what we started, so relax. I'm cool. For some reason, I feel even safer actually being on their side for the moment. I'll be safe until we bring them down."

"What about Queen Fem?" he asked, hoping she had any clue of who she was and her where-abouts.

"Not even close. But trust me. I'm about to go hard and work my way up the ranks. I got the closest I'd ever been to Fields tonight. I just need opportunities like this to impress her. And by any means, I'll take it."

"All right. Just remember, I'm never far. Nobody else knows about you but me. I'm keep-ing it that way, but if need be, under my order, I'll send the big guns to get you out."

"That's it for now. I have to go." She quickly hung up and rapidly began to delete the number as the other motorcycle pulled up behind her.

In the rearview, she eyed her sidekick let the kickstand down, get off, and remove her helmet before shaking her long hair free, until she completed the deletion process. She then stepped out of the Maserati as the bike's headlights shined on both her and the car.

"Good job. Somebody will be here to take it from here," she announced as she walked over toward the bike.

"I got it from here," she told her new cohort. Darkness reclaimed the lot as the two straddled the bike. She took hold of her arms and wrapped them tightly around her waist before she sped away from the drop-off location.

Chapter Eighteen

Starr pulled the Ducati into the long half-circle driveway of the secret minimansion and waited for the four-car garage door to finish elevating. She eased the bike in and waited for the door to shut behind her. She removed the duffel bags from the back of the bike, then hiked them over her shoulders and carried them over to the locked door where she punched an access code into the digital lock pad and it opened. A light beeping sound chimed as she turned to the wall's alarm pad's glowing numbers and keyed in another code. The beeping stopped. She cut the lights off revealing the huge chrome-furnished kitchen with marble floors and a center island with a marble countertop. She set the helmet on the countertop and strutted around, then stared up at the eighteen-foot ceiling's chandelier as she retrieved a bottle of Avian spring water from the fridge. Twisting the top open, Starr took a refreshing sip in an attempt to drink away the migraine she adopted from the night's events.

Her state-of-the-art kitchen illuminated as she walked through it to get to her luxurious onyx graphite-furnished dining room, until she finally reached the dark living room. It was also generously spacious. The ceiling was even higher. The temperature was cool due to the constant lack of body heat. It was usually empty, but this time it wasn't.

Starr tightened her grip on the heavy duffel bags. She made her way toward the long mahogany and cherry wood banister of the marble half-circle, wraparound, double-end staircase.

A voice spoke from the center of the darkness. "Sometimes solving one problem causes another or even more," Queen Fem nonchalantly stated in her infamous articulate robotic tone. Her five foot, 160-pound frame sat seductively in the armless mink loveseat.

Queen Fem's voice caught Starr by surprise. She instantly dropped the duffel bags and drew her registered baby Glock 9 and pointed in Queen Fem's direction all in one swift motion.

Queen Fem seemed to be unfazed by her reaction. "Relax, darling," she calmly stated. "You're going to hurt someone with that thing one of these days." The lamp next to her illuminated, revealing her almond tone.

"That's the point," Starr retorted as her nerves recovered.

Queen Fem flashed a warm smile that lit up her face. She was beautiful as ever. She had just crossed over into a sixth decade, but appeared to be twenty years younger. She was a woman of class. She sat looking calm, non-chalant, sophisticated, and dangerous all in one. Her presence was profoundly demanding. Her attire was tasteful and complemented her voluptuous frame. She wore a silk purple-based multicolored Vera Wang minidress that fit very snug. Her huge diamond-encrusted belt buckle pulled the center of her dress in at her waist-line. Both her breasts and hips protruded in the material. Her manicured, acrylic toes pro-truded perfectly out of the multicolored Jimmy Choo stilettos she wore. Her expensive Indian hair, imported straight from India, was pinned up in a wrap. A single four-carat diamond dan-gled from a tiny platinum chain attached to the lobe of each ear. Her skin was radiant. Her speech reflected extraordinary intellect. Her tongue and lips worked together for proper pronunciation of every single syllable of every word. She spoke clearly and always in the same tone with a steady pattern of an emotionless robot. There she sat with her left leg crossed over her right knee, allowing the heel of her shoe to hang as her foot swayed.

Starr tucked the gun back into the holster attached to her True Religion jeans. "I thought you were going back to bed."

"That was my plan. Things changed. Please, have a seat. Don't be so rude," she ordered more than asked.

Starr sat across from her on the other side of the rectangular aquarium coffee table that sat on the short marble stand. She was on the full-length matching couch. She and Queen Fem locked eyes before Queen Fem broke the silence.

"My insider informed me of the tragic outcome. I assure you that the FBI has no plans of taking this lightly. There's an agent by the name of Tom McCarthy with a real hard-on for us, so to speak. Our message has been sent. We can expect them to reply with force. Be very careful, Starr. My sources also say that there is one of them planted among your side of the organization. Find out who it is and get rid of her. I want her, whoever she may be, shipped back to them in pieces. Her head last," Queen Fem said all in one breathe. Her tone never changed as she spoke.

Queen Fem's words confirmed what the anonymous caller had informed Starr of. She wondered if Queen Fem's source was the same person who had contacted her. She also wondered if Queen Fem had already known she had been contacted by the anonymous caller. Her train of thought was interrupted by Queen Fem's next words.

"I want to tell you a story." Queen Fem extended her arm and gestured for Starr to sit closer. Starr rose and took the seat next to Queen Fem. "There was a father and son bull," Queen Fem began. "They were sitting on top of a hill overlooking a pasture of female cows."

Starr let out a light sigh as Queen Fem told her story. At that moment she felt like a pupil listening to her teacher. She had never respected anyone more or equal to the way she did Queen Fem and she had learned a lot from her throughout the years, but she despised feeling like she was being reprimanded by her mentor the way she knew she was about to be. Still, she gave Queen Fem her undivided attention.

"The son looks down and scans the pasture with excitement in his eyes. He then turns toward his father and says with even more excitement in his tone, 'Dad, look at all those cows. Let's run down there and bed one of them.' The father looks over at the son and smiles, the way a proud parent does to his child. He understands his son's eagerness, his hunger and excitement. But he knows that his son does not know what he knows, just as he didn't when he and his own father sat on top of the very same hill. He reaches out and places his hand on his son's young shoulder and says"—Queen Fem turned to Starr, leaned over and, placing her well-manicured hand on top of Starr's, made eye contact with Starr before she continued—"he says, 'No, son, let's walk down there and bed them all.'"

Starr couldn't help but chuckle a little. She actually enjoyed Queen Fem's story, which was surprising to her.

"Now do you understand why I keep stressing to you that our organization is about control and conquering, not money?" she stated rather than asked. "The money comes along with that."

Starr nodded respectfully. She was appreciative of Queen Fem's wisdom.

"Good." Queen smiled revealing her pearl white teeth, which resembled piano keys, for the first time that evening. "Moving right along," she changed the subject. "Right now, we have their attention. They took us lightly because they thought we were after the streets. Now, they see that's not the case. They now realize who our primary targets are. The same way the Illuminati infiltrated the Masons, the House of Representatives, the U.S. Senate, the Judiciary Committee, and the presidency. It's all done in stages. We will do the same, but with a much more tactical approach. It took them centuries. It will not take us any more than another decade."

"So, what now?" Starr asked as she crossed her own legs and folded her arms under her breasts as she reclined.

"Now, we finally benefit from keeping our hands clean. We will come out of hiding. We will show the world who we really are and what we are made of."

Starr listened with a blank stare plastered across her face.

"Are you with me, my dear?" Queen Fem questioned.

Starr grinned. "Yes, Queen. I'm with you." She made sure to maintain her eye contact with Queen Fem.

"Fabulous! That's my Starr." Queen opened her arms. "Now come over here and give me a kiss."

Once their meeting was done, a limousine escorted by two much older female motorcyclists and choppers pulled back into the half-circle driveway. Queen Fem could hear the familiar engines approaching from inside the miniman-sion. She looked at her watch. "Oh, my time's up. I will be seeing you soon. Do remember everything we've spoken about tonight," she said to Starr.

The two women stood up, hugged, kissed both sides of each other's cheeks, and parted. Queen Fem's heels echoed with every tap on the marble floor until she was back out through the huge foyer. She opened the large, thick oak wood double doors, shut them, and then locked them behind her. She greeted two of the original Double G members, who sat on Harleys, with the wave of her hand as she stepped into the stretch Maybach. The suited female chauffeur gently closed the door after her and then returned to the driver's seat before driving off.

Starr shook her head and smiled as she stared out of the ten-foot window. *She thinks she's the damn queen of England.* She chuckled to herself. She then shut the vertical wall-length thick drapes and went to continue conducting her business. She picked the duffel bag back off the floor and headed upstairs. She entered the master suite and made her way to the safe. She typed in the access code and a tiny bulb switched colors from red to green. Starr swung the door open and transferred the money from the bag to the vault. When she was done, she locked it back up and exited the hidden room. Only two people knew about the storage room: she and Queen Fem.

Starr made her way back downstairs. It had been a long day and an even longer night. All she wanted now was to climb in her bed and rest her mind. With those being her thoughts, she made her way back in which she had come. Just as she exited the house her text message alert vibrated against her hip. She smiled when she saw who the text was from. In an instant, she changed her plans. There was no doubt in her mind now that she wouldn't be getting any rest tonight. And she was fine with that because she knew she had some making up to do.

Chapter Nineteen

Salty's Bar & Grill was at the corner of the same block as Club Panties. It was open twenty-four hours, seven days a week. Although it was a tavern, the setting was very classy. Bubbles and Monica sat in the back section at a secluded table, drinking liquor and eating while getting to know each other better.

"So, tell me. How did you get in?" Monica asked as she nibbled away at her cheeseburger and large order of potato wedges. She took a sip of her rum and Coke to wash it down.

Bubbles cracked a wide smile, blushing as she lowered her voice. "Well, you know we're not supposed to tell, but, it's just us here, right?" She flashed Monica a trusting smile. "So anyway, I'm originally from North Las Vegas, but went away to school after I graduated to California. I moved back out here after I dropped out of LSU thinking this guy, who I had a crush on since I was a young girl wet behind the ears, would be interested in kickin' it with me. It didn't work out that way though. By the time I came back he was even deeper in the streets than when I left and became an even bigger asshole, at least to me anyway."

"Have you ever, you know, with a guy, since you been a Double G?" Monica shyly asked.

Bubbles's face wrinkled up with apparent disgust. "A loooong time ago, and I do mean long time," she emphasized. "Actually he was my first and last," Bubbles confessed. "That's like the first commandment of the Double Gs." She lowered her tone back into a quiet whisper while leaning forward as if she was about to tell a ghost story. "They say that once you're in, if Queen Fem or Starr even suspects that you've been with a man or even heard the rumor, you get sent to the OBGYN to get checked out. You get one pass during your initiation because they know you may have to seal the deal to convince the target. After that, if it ain't tight down there, you get terminated for the violation," Bubbles revealed.

Monica tried her hardest not to make any reaction to Bubbles's last statement, but she was sure she had done a poor job. Bubbles had noticed the change in her facial expression.

"Oh God. I hope you haven't."

"Who? Never," Monica lied, defending her cover.

"Oh, I was about to say," Bubbles continued, "So, anyway, I was bored one day and I'm out just club hoppin'. I was tore up from the floor up, you hear me." Bubbles laughed as she reminisced. "So, I don't know if I did or not, but the taxi driver said I told him to take me to a strip club. The MF assumed I was gay and took me to Club Panties. I'm not sure if it was the liquor or what, but I had a ball. There were women all shapes, sizes, and colors in there, a lot who looked like me." Bubbles used her hands to demonstrate she referred to her weight size.

"That night women were hittin' on me left and right and it felt good and different and it excited me. After a while I kept hearing stuff about a crew called the Double Gs. I became real interested, so eventually I started doing research there on my own. Rumors were circulating that they screened everyone who regularly attended, so I began auditioning. I was doing whatever it took to get noticed. And then one day I was approached by a mysterious woman who slipped me a card and told me to go over to Treasures and tend bar. Felicia was my trainer. She was very patient with me. I was so overanxious that I kept fuckin' it up for weeks until one night I finally got it right, and then I got my assignment." Bubbles paused. "Well, my real assignment, anyway."

"What do you mean by that?" Bubbles had lost her.

"My initial initiation was personal not business," Bubbles confessed, as she thought about how long ago that had been since Chase and how far she had come. She had grown so much as a woman and a Double G.

"I'm confused." A peculiar look appeared on Monica's face.

"Let's just say that my childhood crush is over." Bubbles winked. "But, anyway," she then continued, "my first business assignment was a white crooked cop." A sinister smile popped up out of nowhere as Bubbles took a trip down memory lane. "His name was Officer Blake and he had a real weakness for young black hookers, particularly voluptuous ones." She giggled like a schoolgirl. "Every chance he got, he picked one up. He would take them to the same old run-down motel. Most of the dancers who moonlighted outside the club already knew him. He would always go after the new ones.

"So, I dressed up and played the part. I'll never forget I had on a white halter top that was cut to stop at the underside of my breasts while my cleavage burst out above." Bubbles chuckled at the memory. "And I had on a black and red checker-print miniskirt that stopped at the under cuff of my ass cheeks. I wore a pair of multicolored Christian Dior leggings underneath and knee-high boots. My hair was in two pigtails, one on each side, and I was sucking on a lollipop, looking like a young schoolgirl. The phone they gave me was in my Prada purse. That was it. I didn't have a weapon or anything. I just stayed out there, waiting for him while I blended in with the other girls who were working the boulevard.

"It didn't take long," she remembered. "A couple of hours after his shift was over, he finally rolled up in his Dodge Charger. Without hesitation, he pointed straight at me. I pretended not to notice him. I was bending over, talking to some old white pervert in another car, giving Officer Blake the full back view of all this ass. He was wide open. He waited for me to finish flirting before he called me over. I leaned in his window with my cleavage in his face, sucking the Blow Pop, and introduced myself as Candy. He instructed me to get in and immediately handed me a hundred and a fifty dollar bill and then he whipped out his li'l pecker before even pulling off. He reached for my Blow Pop and snatched it out of my mouth. After he threw it out of the window he grabbed the back of my head with the same hand and informed me that now I had

something new to suck on with a li'l mo' flava."
Bubbles shook her head and snickered.

"But anyway, I did it nice an' slow, all the way
to the raggedy-ass motel, but I made sure he
didn't cum. He already had a set of keys for this
hole-in-the-wall room. I followed him in there.
He had his police uniform folded up on his chair
with all of the normal accessories sitting on top.
I pretended to be excited and told him that I
wanted to play a game. I played the li'l schoolgirl
act real well. He wasn't up to it at first, but I
stepped into him and began massaging his little
pink balls. And then I dropped to my knees and
began sucking his li'l dick again until he agreed.
I nearly threw up. He had all this pubic hair that
smelled like a fuckin' wet dog." Bubbles frowned
as she relived the scene.

"I jumped back up to my feet, but I kept his
pants down. Everything in there was made out
of some old-ass wood. I sat him down in this
piece of shit chair. The seat was made out of
some type of straw. It scratched his skin up at
first, but he seemed to like it. I told him to stay
right there and I seductively stripped down and
put on his uniform. Needless to say, it turned
him on. I told him that he was the robber I just
caught and I would have to interrogate him to
get all the information I needed to make an

arrest. He started smiling and getting even more aroused and erect. I knew I had him. I took the two little nylon ribbons from my pigtails and used them to tie up each of his feet to the front legs of the chair real tight. And then I handcuffed both of his wrists to the pegs in the back of the chair. He couldn't move for shit." She giggled.

"Then came the big surprise. I kicked the chair over on its side. It took him down along with it. He was lying flat on his side, still in the sitting position. He started cursing up a storm so much that I had to use my panties to gag his mouth. I took the small pocket knife from his keychain and used it to cut the bottom of the chair out. And being that his pants was still down, there it was, his whole little red asshole. Gurrrl." Bubbles dragged her word and doubled over with laughter. "He started sweatin' so hard on that rusty-ass carpet. I took his nightstick and got on my knees. A sudden rush of adrenaline came over me. I started plunging the shit out his ass. Remember what happened to that African in Harlem back in the day? What was his name?" she rhetorically asked, not really expecting Monica to answer.

"Luima," Monica clarified, paying full attention.

"Yeah, him. So, anyway, I began fuckin' the shit outta him with that damn billy club and then I pulled it out. It had feces and blood all over it. He had been screaming for his life. I crawled around the front of his red, sweaty face, ungagged him and shoved the nightstick in his mouth while reminding him that I wasn't the only one with somethin' new to suck on that had a li'l mo' flava. He threw up all over me. That made me really mad. Then it hit me. Just when I thought I was finished with my mission, I realized I forgot somethin'. Gurrrl." You could literally see all thirty-two teeth in Bubbles's mouth as she smiled from ear to ear, thinking about the ordeal.

"What?" Monica wanted to know. She was all ears.

"I ain't record shit that had happened!" she exclaimed. She looked around making sure no one was paying them any mind. Her voice had carried a little bit too much for her taste.

"Are you serious?" Monica's eyes widened.

"As a heart attack." Bubbles chuckled.

"So, what did you do?" Monica asked the obvious question.

"What do you think?" Bubbles shot her a distorted look. "I had to do it to him all over again." She said it matter-of-factly, right before they both burst out laughing until tears filled their eyes.

"Gurrrl, yo' ass is crazy!" Monica proclaimed while the hysteria filled her gut.

Bubbles continued, "Shit. That ain't the half. I left him that damn memo. Come ta find out, I pulled off a two for one. By us blackmailing him and sending him on missions, we got his partner, too. And they both crooked as a lightning bolt. So, his partner was forced to ride it out with him or they were both goin' down. Damn."

"So, anyway, how'd yours go? I saw who you left with. It was about to go down that night. Freeze was straight trippin'. He probably felt he had something to prove since the twins got his ass. Prime is much more smarter than he is though. But don't let that smooth, pretty boy diplomatic act fool you. He's a dangerous dude. How'd you get him?"

Monica paused for a long second, trying to mentally recall the footage of the rehearsed video they made. But she highly doubted she could explain the fake story as vividly as Bubbles had just done. She decided to buy herself some time to get her story together.

"It's boring as fuck, compared to yours. But I'll tell you all about mine after you tell me about the personal one."

Bubbles's mood suddenly changed. "Nothing to talk about." She brushed Monica's request off. Even when she had first mentioned it, it made her feel some type of way.

Monica picked up on it. It made her want to know. Still she trod lightly. "It's okay. I understand if it's too personal for you to talk about."

"He was my first love," Bubbles blurted out. "Hell, my only love." She added a light chuckle.

"Aww." Monica lit up.

"Don't aww. He was a fucking dick," Bubbles informed her.

Monica wiped the dreamy look off of her face. "My bad," she apologized.

"Naw, it's cool. You didn't know," Bubbles accepted. "But, yeah, he used to treat me like shit, when we were kids." She looked around the semi-crowded room as she spoke.

Monica listened attentively.

"We grew up together in Carey Arms apartments."

The mentioning of the housing projects caught Monica's attention. Her older half brother was from there. The two had the same father but her mother was cool most of the time with him coming around to visit occasionally. She was twelve years old when she had received the news that he was found dead in an apartment on the outskirts of the city limits. He was nineteen. Although they didn't see one another much, when they did it was nothing but love. The two were close. Some of her fondest childhood memories were of when he would come and visit her. There was never a time she could recall that he came to see her without bearing gifts. She loved how he used to always stay long enough to help her with her homework and always made sure no one was picking on her in or out of school. She took his death hard. In her eyes, he was the best brother a little sister could have. It wasn't until later that she found out about his dark side. Because there was cocaine found in the apartment he was found in, police ruled it as a drug deal gone bad. But the way it was said he was found and killed raised eyebrows among her family. His death was the reason why she had chosen her career path. She was so impacted by the death of her older brother that she made a vow when she was a senior in high school that she would seek justice for him. Bubbles's story made her think about him as she listened.

"As kids, we did everything together and he used to always have my back. At least, until he started feelin' his self." Bubbles scowled. "I remember this one particular time, I was just coming home from school and I guess he had just bought his new car." Bubbles stared off at nothing in particular. "Shit, it was so long ago, I don't even remember what kind it was. I think it was a BMW."

Monica could feel her heart rate increasing. *It can't be,* she thought. At the time of her brother's death, he too had a BMW. The last time she had seen him, he had taken her for a ride to the corner store in his candy apple red 325i. She could hear his voice in her head as he explained the difference between his 325i and the 318is. Back then at the young age of twelve, she couldn't care less. All she knew was that her big brother had a fly ride and she was riding in it. Now, knowing the make meant everything to her. Her muscles tensed as she shifted her weight from left to right. That was the side where her gun was tucked. *I swear to God this bitch better not say it was a 325i,* Monica thought. She sat on pins and needles as Bubbles seemed to struggle with remembering the make of the car. Then, all of a sudden, a look of remembrance appeared on her face.

Monica's adrenaline began to pump.

"Yeah, it was a BMW. A 3—" Before she could spit it out, a loud smack on her back caused her to choke on her own words.

"What you two hoes gossiping about?" Felicia chimed in. She had appeared out of nowhere. She chuckled at Bubbles's reaction to her introduction of smacking her on the back.

Bubbles shook her head and flashed a smile. "Bitch, you tryin'a kill me?" she spat in between laughter.

"I love you too, baby girl," Felicia replied with a huge grin.

"Hey, Fe." She knew Felicia was only being herself and she loved her for who she was.

Monica's smile on the other hand was a forced one. She was steaming inside. She never got to get the confirmation of the type of BMW Bubbles's childhood sweetheart drove. She knew back then everybody from pimps to hustlers pushed the same type of rides. During the time of her brother's murder, there were over two dozen BMW 325i and 318is owners in the Carey Arms apartment. Knowing that Bubbles's victim's BMW was a 3 Series was not solid enough for her. She needed the specific make or the name of the victim. With more time, she was sure she could have gotten what she needed. Had it not been for Felicia, she would have had the opportunity.

Fucking bitch, she cursed Felicia in her head. She wanted to smack the shit out of her. Since the day she and Felicia came to Starr's aid, there had been an uncomfortable silence between the two. She knew she was now one of them, but there was something about that day that left her feeling a little uneasy.

"What the hell's wrong with you?" Felicia asked her.

She was surprised behind her question. "Nothing." Monica cleared her throat. "Why'd you ask that?"

"Because, you look like you got something stuck up all that ass of yours," Felicia retorted with a straight face.

Bubbles nearly spat out her drink she had just taken a sip of. She was about to respond, but her attention was drawn to the pair who just walked in the establishment.

"Look, there are the twins!" she blurted as she waved Glitter and Sparkle over.

The twins strutted in their direction, looking fly as ever, stunting with their Vanson motorcycle jackets on. The Double G symbol was flooded with diamonds. Heads turned as their shapely hips and firm, thick asses swayed from left to right and bounced up and down. Glitter's ass cheeks shook like Jell-O shots in her black leggings while Sparkle's fought to bust out of the skintight blue jeans she wore.

"Now, them some gangsta bitches for yo' ass, right there!" Felicia praised. "Born to be Double Gs."

"So, you don't think it could be them?" Bubbles inquired in regard to having an informant in their organization. She intentionally left out what she was referring to due to Monica's presence. Felicia was well aware of what she meant.

"Nah, not them two. They were built for this. Some chicks you just know," Felicia vouched for the twins. "I'd pick this bitch before I pick them," she added in reference to Monica. "Besides, they passed the poly."

"Pick me for what?" Monica asked in a puzzled manner.

Bubbles shook her head and let out a light chuckle. "Don't worry about what she talkin' about," Bubbles offered.

Felicia just laughed. Unbeknownst to them both, Monica was not as clueless as they thought. She had overheard some of the Double Gs talking about a possible snitch in the crew and figured that's what Bubbles and Felicia were referring to. None of the new Double Gs were privy to the Ovary Office meetings while on probation, which was why Monica was not in attendance when Starr had given the polygraph test she knew

Felicia was referring to. It was the same day she had actually been given her mission.

"Wassup, Gs?" Sparkle and Glitter sang in unison, joining the other Double Gs. They both took turns hugging Felicia, Bubbles, and Monica.

"What y'all up to?" Felicia asked.

"Tryin'a find a way to earn our keep and stay afloat at the same time since we ain't at the club no more," Sparkle replied.

"Don't worry about earning y'all keep. Y'all straight for now." Felicia stuck her hand in her navy business suit pants front pocket and pulled out all the money she had in her pocket. "Give me a minute, I'll have something lined up for y'all. Until then, y'all bust this down." She handed Sparkle the stack of hundreds.

"We appreciate it, big sis," Glitter spoke on their behalf. She was sure the money her sister had just accepted was at least $4,000.

Bubbles stood up out of her chair and shoved her hand into her pocket. "Here. Y'all gonna need more than that." She handed all she had to Glitter. "A bitch gotta eat. After all, I know it takes a lot to keep this shit right." Bubbles grabbed a handful of Glitter's ass then released it and gave it a smack.

"You know it." Glitter smiled. They all joined each other in laughter at Bubbles's comment and actions.

Felicia's ended abruptly. Her sudden frown caught the Double Gs' attention immediately. They all followed the direction her eyes were focused on.

"Ain't that Prime's young boy?" Bubbles asked, already knowing the answer to her question. She knew who the young goons were who had just entered the building.

"Yeah, that's that li'l clown-ass nigga," Felicia snarled.

Young Clips came ditty bopping through the door with his crew of young menaces to society. He scanned the tavern and the first face he noticed was Felicia's. He flashed a schoolboy smile hoping she would return the gesture. Instead, all he received was a pair of rolled eyes.

"Girl, let's get up outta here 'fore I have to fuck this li'l stalker up," she said. She could already feel her temperature rising. Lately, Young Clips had become a nuisance she was growing tired of.

Monica recognized some of the faces from the night the two crews at the club were about to get into it.

"What's that all about?" Bubbles asked Felicia.

"It really ain't about nothin', but he gonna wind up makin' it something. I'll tell you when we get to the spot," was what Felicia offered.

"We gonna hang here," Glitter opted. "We'll catch up with y'all later."

Felicia, Bubbles, and Monica nodded. "Lunch on y'all today, too." Felicia flashed a smirk.

The twins smiled. "Got you." Glitter winked.

"Let's get the fuck outta here." Felicia waved them on.

Both Bubbles and Monica rose and followed as she navigated her way toward the exit. Bubbles ignored Young Clips as they floated passed him. Monica, on the other hand, watched as Felicia and Young Clips made eye contact. Young Clips had on the same smile he had plastered across his face since he had entered the spot. Monica was sure Felicia was not smiling. Although she couldn't stop thinking about Bubbles's story, she couldn't help but notice something odd between Felicia and Young Clips. She made a mental note of the incident.

Chapter Twenty

The warm, early morning sunshine spilled into the high-rise office of Special Agent McCarthy, who was asleep at his desk. His face was buried into his folded arms. There was a light knock before the wood grain door slowly swung ajar. He was in such a slumber he never bothered to look up to see who had just entered the room.

Chief Andrews stuck his head in first, and then allowed his body to follow. "No sleeping on the job!" He tossed the joke into the air, startling Agent McCarthy who quickly sat up, forgetting where he was. And then it registered. The files on his desk jogged his memory.

"Chief Andrews, what brings you here, and so early?" Agent McCarthy asked after catching a quick glimpse at his wall clock. It was barely 7:15 a.m.

"This!" Chief Andrews waved the folded newspaper before tossing it onto McCarthy's desk. The front page fell open flat. "I heard about it and then I read about it."

"Holy shit!" Agent McCarthy yelled. He sprang up and leaned over with both hands planted into the desk. "How? Who?"

"A leak maybe?" Chief Andrews suggested.

The headline read, FEDERAL AGENTS SLAIN BY FEMALE GANG. There was a full picture beneath it, showing a perfect view of the tragic crime scene. Agent McCarthy took a closer look.

"Wait. This isn't an inside leak. They must've photographed what happened and sent it to the papers. Look." Agent McCarthy spun the newspaper upside down and into Chief Andrews's direction while pointing. "Think about it. How was such a clear photo taken? The press wasn't anywhere near there. The entire incident was to be kept under wraps until we knew exactly what happened."

"So, they did it. Bold," Chief Andrews smoothly stated.

"It's a damn slap in the face. That's what it is. Two agents under the age of thirty are dead. Don't you dare give 'em any credit. They'll burn in hell when I catch 'em!"

"Hey, I'm on your side, big guy. I stopped by to let you know I'm here to help. This is spreading news through all law enforcement. Everyone's paying full attention now. No more jokes. It's war. That could've been any one of us out there dead."

The last statement deflated Agent McCarthy. He flopped back down into his chair and buried his face into the palms of his hands. "No, that's the problem. It couldn't have been. It was them under my command. I forced them to go by taking advantage of their low ranks, forgetting that this isn't about that. I was supposed to send the most skillful and tactical agents out into the field. This isn't the local authorities. We leave our weak back in the office. Only our strong go out in the field of hunting."

The conversation was interrupted by Agent McCarthy's secretary peeking her head into the door with a stack of folders pressed against her breast. "Agent McCarthy, they have the tape cued up and ready. They're waiting for you in the situation room."

"Great, Mandy. Thank you. Let them know I'm on my way." Agent McCarthy looked back up at his wall clock in amazement. It shocked him that people were in so early. He stood up, grabbed the suit jacket off the back of his chair, and swung his arms into it while footing his way around the desk. "You're free to join us," he stated to Chief Andrews.

The situation room was packed. It was a large, comfortable room with a long, oval cherry wood table that seated twenty agents on high-quality leather chairs. Glasses of water or cups of coffee sat in front of them next to their folders. Some were open. Some were still closed. Each agent had a look on their face that showed they meant business. They were up early, suited and, most of all, serious. Especially Agent Snyder, who was sitting up front.

A large screen mechanically lowered from the ceiling as the high-tech electrical blinds closed by remote, darkening the room just as Agent McCarthy walked in. Not a single sound was made. All of the seats were taken. Chief Andrews stood next to a few of the remaining agents in the back. On Agent McCarthy's signal, the dashboard's digital footage began to play both video and audio.

The scene started from when Starr had originally left Club Panties and loaded the duffel bag into her car. Agent McCarthy aimed the remote at the CD reader and fast-forwarded to the highway scene. At first, it all seemed so calm. It was as if there wasn't any way Starr should've made the tail on her. Agent Mullin had kept it textbook. Agent McCarthy noticed the trucks closing in on the agents. Not much could be seen from the dashboard camera's view but, between that and the audio, it all told a story that came together, leaving the imagination to handle the rest.

Glass could be heard shattering. Flesh being ripped, screams being yelled, it all happened so fast. The agents viewing the footage were in shock as they watched five trucks of different kinds with no license plates flee, leaving the slightest glimpse of Starr's tail lights up ahead right before the screen seemed to start tumbling after a loud bang. The car was flipping and then it stopped. The dash cam occasionally caught shots of the motorcycles slowing down as the screen froze.

Agent McCarthy caught his best shot at the two motorcycles with armed passengers on the back heading to the Impala to daringly finish the job. He pressed the save button on the remote control and then continued the video. All that could be seen was smoke rising through the headlights that reflected off the rusty gray guardrail the Impala smashed into when it landed upright.

A few seconds later, the motorcycles could be heard ripping away. The lights in the situation room came back on. All of the agents were blown away. Emotions ran high within the room. Everyone felt it. As silence tried to set in, ties were being loosened, throats were being cleared, tears were restrained; most of all, jokes were deeply regretted. Agent McCarthy was choked up the most. He lightly coughed into his balled fist before he spoke.

"Ladies and gentlemen, I believe that we've just caught two of the biggest breaks ever. Sadly, it was at the expense of the lives of two young agents. If we fail now, we fail them. Their sacrifice would be for nothing. We've just witnessed their devout bravery, all the way down to the end. Let's never forget that. Now, we have a good shot here." The still photos he had saved appeared on the screen. Each of the girls' bodacious bodies were draped in all black.

"Our mission is to get a lead on them damn trucks!" Agent McCarthy screamed with emotion.

Just then a skinny, middle-aged white agent raised his hand high into the air. An ink pen was pinched between his thumb and index finger as he held it high. He bore red freckles that were partially covered by his thin glasses. A tiny red light was blinking from the side of the Bluetooth headset in his left ear. A small laptop was flipped open in front of him.

Agent McCarthy snapped at him for his rude interruption. "What?"

Agent Homer began to speak in a nervous tone. All eyes were on him as he responded.

"Actually, sir, I tracked the route they were on and cross-referenced it with the time that was at the bottom of the video's screen along with all gas station surveillance near all exits and tollbooths in the direction they were headed."

"Good work. Now, get to the point!" Agent McCarthy demanded in a firm but calm tone. Even as a law enforcement agent, he hated mystery. Especially being so close to the edge of it.

"Well, just up ahead, at that speed and direction, I figured they would've run into a tollbooth at some point, which they did."

"And?"

"And, sir, while I was sitting here, I took the liberty of calling the nearest tollbooths and requested the footage from their surveillance cameras around that time."

"And?" Agent McCarthy was visibly frustrated beyond belief. "Get to the point, Agent!" he snapped.

"Oh, sir. They have footage of all five trucks coming through around that time. It seemed to be all women drivers in disguises. At first, they wanted a warrant, but in light of the public mockery of the agents' murders, they were willing to help. They're faxing the photos as we speak."

At that point, the fax machine in the upfront corner of the room beeped as five photos came through. Agent McCarthy retrieved them quickly and looked over at Agent Homer.

"You're getting one hell of a raise!" he yelled. He reviewed the still frames. Only one picture was clear as day. One of the women was paying the toll without her disguise. Agent McCarthy smacked the paper with the back of his hand.

"Gotcha," he uttered, as he passed the photo around the room.

Chapter Twenty-one

Young Clips was determined to come up in the world. He was only nineteen years old, but he had been under Prime's wing since he was barely thirteen and during those six years he had accomplished a lot, more than anyone expected, but still not enough for him. He felt he was still looked at as a kid, especially by Felicia. Whenever he would purposely just happen to run into her out of the blue, she would brush him off, claiming that he was still in diapers. Even worse, she would remind him of her sexual preference and declare that he wasn't making enough money to make her even think about changing her mind. Felicia may have been on the other side of the fence, but Young Clips was not convinced that's where she wanted to be. He was in love with her at first sight, denying it to himself that it was stalking. He followed her every chance he got, especially from work, just to be able to make it look like they happened to bump into each other. He had familiarized himself with her patterns and routines.

Young Clips always suspected Felicia to be an elite Double G member with status. But after following her around for a few weeks, he had learned more than he was looking to know. What he knew thus far was powerful. He kept it all to himself though. There were times when he was ready to fill Prime and the rest of the crew in on the details; but, for one, they would clown him for stalking and, two, they would never take him seriously. So, he was just waiting for the right time to see which way he would tip the scale to his advantage. The leverage was certainly there and timing was everything, he knew.

Born Christian Reeves, Young Clips was quite tall for his age, but was always thin and lanky. He wore all of his clothes twice his size. His wardrobe never differed. It was fitting for his lifestyle: a thick black Champion hoodie, no matter what the weather was, baggy black jeans that sagged low up under his ass, and two twin .45s on his waist. The only thing that varied was the either black or tan construction Timberlands on his feet. He had a pure baby face with a slightly oversized nose. He kept the same cornrows in for months at a time. Still, his personal hygiene stayed on point. Living such a filthy lifestyle influenced him to shower at least twice a day.

After meeting Prime, Young Clip's future definitely became brighter than his past. From the age of six, Young Clips was raised in a foster home after being a ward of the state. His mother was a drug addict who couldn't even take care of herself, and his father, who he had never gotten a chance to meet, was serving a life sentence in state prison for several murders. By the time Young Clips was thirteen, he left and turned to the streets, where he ran with other kids slightly older than him. He shuffled houses among them all. Some had to sneak him in, but with an untrusting eye. It was because he always looked like he was up to something devious. Most of the time he was, but only in the streets. He prided himself on being loyal, and stayed true to anyone who genuinely considered him as a friend. Back then, he and his snot-nosed, ashy-face bandits formed a mischievous gang called the Alley Cats. They were extremely young, but lawless. They hung out in front of a Laundromat, which was a heavy drug strip owned by Prime.

Prince was the silent enforcer. It was well known that whenever Prince was called on to get involved, it was too late for the opposition.

Yet and still, these young teens were in their own world, not caring about what was going on up the street. They stayed down on their end, terrorizing everyone who came through, eventually running the drug money away to the other side of town, which was looking more organized. C-Class had been watching what was going on for a few weeks before he, along with Prince, decided to step to them.

The Alley Cats were in front of the Laundromat, slap boxing, smoking, drinking, and playing music on a portable boom box, just having a good time. The radio was sitting high on top of the payphone stand. Young Clips was sitting next to it on a milk crate with his arms folded across his chest and his hoodie drowning his head. A mix CD had them all amped up. It was seven at night. The sun was just setting, but it was still light outside. Young Clips was staring down at the filth-stained, chipped-up pavement while mentally rapping along with the words. He was in his own zone. Then it happened, right next to him. The most adrenaline-rushing sound he had ever heard. The sweetness of it ran through his veins as he just sat there without flinching absorbing the aftermath of the echo. The shell casing tapping the ground was pleasing.

The music had stopped, violently disrupted. The Panasonic boom box had been blown to pieces. Shattered hard plastic splattered all over the young teens like bomb shrapnel on a group of soldiers. There was a slight pause of silence and shock and then everybody ran except for Young Clips. He stayed in the same exact position, but slowly lifted his head up and leaned back against the brick wall behind him, still rapping the remaining words under his breath.

C-Class smiled at Prince, whose face was pure stone with the smoking gun still in his hand.

"Oh, so you got heart, huh? You ain't gonna scatter away with the rest of them?"

Young Clips slowly turned to C-Class's direction while using his right hand to swipe the hoodie away from obstructing his view. "For what? The captain goes down with the ship. I ain't scared. I ain't do nothin' wrong. Oh, by the way, that's forty-six dollars for the radio, four dollars for the batteries, ten dollars for the CD, and a hundred dollars for wasting my time." He nonchalantly stuck his left hand out while using his right to swipe his hoodie back down over his head as he closed his eyes, relaxed, and waited for payment. He was dead serious.

C-Class turned to face Prince, still smiling. "You heard him. Pay the young man."

On demand, Prince removed a thick knot of money from his pocket and flicked his thumb before slowly peeling off two hundred-dollar bills. He folded them the long way and then extended them out to touch Young Clips's fingertips. As soon as he did, he swiftly kicked the crate out from under Young Clips's ass while trying to jerk the money back. But it was too late. Not only did Young Clips snatch the money, he was still in the sitting position even with the crate gone. He was prepared. He spoke in a low, steady tone as he stood up straight, tucking the money into his pocket.

"I'm going to forget that you did that." He turned to Prince and pulled his hoodie back again to expose his entire face, locking eyes, showing no signs of fear. "Only because the crate wasn't mine. But you just tried to renege on a deal. If you wasn't gonna pay me, you should have just said so. Maybe if you would come at me like a man, we could've worked somethin' out. But you didn't give me the opportunity. You assumed that because I'm young, you could bully me or scare me away like you think you did my squad. Nah, I used to admire y'all. I was down here studying y'all and how y'all move up there. Y'all had music blasting from your cars; all we could afford was that boom box you just destroyed. Y'all got that barbershop up there, we got the Laundromat. Y'all stick together and don't take shit from nobody; neither do we."

As Young Clips stated that, the Alley Cats were slowly returning. But instead of being bunched up together, they were in strategically placed positions all throughout the entire block and the side streets. They each had a weapon of some sort. A few even had guns. They were slowly creeping and closing in, staying low behind cars and riding the walls of the brick buildings. C-Class and Prince couldn't believe it. Young Clips had never broken eye contact with Prince. It was as if he knew his crew was coming back, and strong, but didn't need them to show his heart.

He continued, "Now, I see things different and I'm lettin' this slide. This one is on me." Young Clips removed the two hundred-dollars bills from his pocket and set them down on the payphone. "The boom box wasn't mines either. I took it from somebody. Right out of his hands, straight up, no weapon. And I had my gun on me when I did it." Young Clips lifted the bottom of his sweatshirt up to reveal his pistol. "But he never saw it. We'll just call this karma."

And just like that, Young Clips turned his back on C-Class and Prince and walked away, never allowing them to say a word. He stuck two fingers into his mouth and blew out a sharply loud coded whistle into the air. All of the Alley

Cats came out of their positions and flocked around him as they disappeared.

Prime couldn't believe a word of the tickling story. He laughed so hard as C-Class and Prince told it play by play, word for word.

"Uh-uh. Young'un's like twelve. He ain't talkin' like that. That's grown man shit. And he was right. You should've known betta, Prince. Y'all could've made ya own block hot with that bullshit. Radios don't shoot back. Y'all gotta get shit in order. Preteens can't be runnin' us outta business," he seriously joked. They were sitting in Prime's restaurant, eating at a private table in the back.

"Young'un got heart, PM. He's smart. He got them otha li'l niggas brainwashed. And I swear he's the youngest," C-Class added.

Prime's fork sounded off as it dropped down into the glass plate. He got serious as he spoke to both of his top men. "Listen. He ain't got them brainwashed. He got them all on the same page and in order. Just like us. It's the same situation. Them li'l niggas are so young and advanced they're willing to die for their respect. And they're smart. They moved in silence. Young Clips was the sacrificial lamb of distraction and diversion. Y'all assumed that his crew ran away out of fear, because not one of them threatened y'all while fleeing. Young Clips held y'all there, knowing they'd be back strong, just as I would've done. It was all mapped out. They forced y'all to come to them and to respect them by the time they left. They knew your move. Y'all were a step behind. It was a game of chess. They put y'all in check and spared the mate. Where's young'un at? I'm gonna go find him."

"And what?" C-Class asked.

"And give him a position. The biggest part of this picture is that most likely his pockets were empty, but he still returned the money. To me, that says more about him than anything."

The next day, as always, after learning from his mistakes, Young Clips stepped his game up. Instead of a crate he was sitting on an old, rusted steel dining room table chair that had been thrown out. It would've been impossible to get kicked from under him. He and his crew all chipped in to buy a new radio this time, and a Young Money mix CD. Young Clips had on his usual black attire. His head was drowned by his hoodie while he focused on devouring his favorite meal: Chinese food. In a single moment, it seemed as if all the breath around him was lost in silence as his crew gasped, leaving only the radio playing. Young Clips looked up to see the cause and almost choked on a chicken bone he was sucking clean.

A powder blue Bentley GT had pulled up and parked right in front of the Laundromat's chipped, unlevel sidewalk and parked next to a huge pile of stinking black garbage bags. The horn honked twice as the window rolled down.

"Get in," Prime ordered.

Everyone looked down at Young Clips. He looked around with an odd look plastered on his face as if Prime was speaking to someone else.

"Yeah, you!" Prime confirmed.

"I'm eatin'!" Young Clips shouted while dipping his fingers into the white foam tray, dripping with sauce and grease.

"I can see that. That's why you're gonna use them napkins in that paper bag and wipe your hands clean before you get in my ride," Prime declared.

Young Clips thought about contesting but he was curious, so he opened up the bottle of Fiji spring water and poured it onto his hands before drying them off with his napkins.

"Watch my food, y'all," he ordered as he bopped to the car and reached for the door handle. It was locked as he tried to pull it open and grew angry. "What kinda games you playin'?" he aggressively questioned.

Prime stared him down with intense scrutiny. "Go clean yourself up and come back correct. Then you get in."

Clips caught on. He walked back into the huddle of his crew and passed his .32 automatic off to his right-hand man. As he returned to the vehicle, he heard a double click and he entered. The window slowly rolled back up as they pulled off.

"Wassup?" Young Clips asked.

"I got a job for you and your team. But I'm only hiring you. You're hiring them. That's how business works. You're the boss. You handle your own payroll. Make it work however you can; just get the job done," Prime testified, keeping his eyes on the road.

"First of all, how do you know I—"

Prime cut Young Clips off. "Five hundred a week. Every Friday at nine p.m. I already got you your own apartment. It's a furnished three-bed-room. Keep the noise down and stay low. Don't shit where you sleep. Bring your top three men with you. One of y'all sleep on the couch a different night in rotation to watch the door. A king always protects his castle. Even himself. Now, your job is to spread your team out. I'm gonna give you a printout of all the streets I own. I want all four corners of them sealed off at all times. Now y'all will be sealing money in instead of chasing it out. But y'all won't touch the product. It's just steering and security. Any of y'all see anything out of order, report it directly to Prince, C-Class, or me. It starts tonight, clear?" he asked as he pulled put seven hundred-dollar bills and passed them to Young Clips.

Young Clips counted out five of them and handed Prime back the other two. "You said five hundred."

Prime smiled to himself knowing he made the right decision. He waved the money back off. "Nah, that's for Prince. Never start business off on a dirty slate. The dust from the chalk smears too easily. Pretty soon, you can't tell what's there and what's been erased."

By the time Young Clips had turned sixteen, he was "made." The team of Alley Cats perfected their structure and solidified themselves as up-and-coming terrorists. Anything that got in their way was moved. Nothing came close to disrupting Prime's operation. In fact, the money started coming in twice as much. Their friends were treated as clients. They were safely escorted up and down the blocks. That earned him respect and admiration among his crew and made drug users more comfortable spending their money on the particular block. Every day, Young Clips managed to impress Prime by doing something smart or admirable in the streets.

Young Clips finally got the opportunity he was waiting for. He had upgraded to twin .45s and was itching to use them. The money wasn't enough. He was an adrenaline junky. He wanted the rush from the power. Prime became his idol; he had graduated to just being an overseer. He hung around C-Class and Prince down at the barbershop while his team either walked around, drove around in cars, or used bicycles, motorcycles, or dirt bikes. The Alley Cats grew over sixty deep. And all of them ate well. The scraps were enough to keep them content with just being outside regulating and flirting with girls.

C-Class and Prince were shooting dice outside of the barbershop while Prime was inside getting razor lined. He was facing the two huge outside windows. He never allowed the barber to obstruct his view. Not even for a second. A split second was a man's worst enemy, Prime believed.

Outsiders were welcome to join the dice game. Young Clips was sitting in the driver's seat of Prince's 750Li listening to Biggie's "Niggas Bleed" while he smoked a blunt. While rapping along to every syllable, he heard a commotion break out. He looked to his right and could see C-Class arguing, but couldn't make out the words, so he looked into the barbershop's window and made eye contact with Prime. They both shook their heads.

C-Class was arguing with an older man about whether he had to pay for shooting the same number that C-Class had rolled. C-Class was flipping. "My muthafukin' bank, my muthafuckin' rules. Pushers pay, trips pay double. Cracks and leaning dice are good, as long as you can stack 'em. Closest numba to the sky. You see it, you pay it! My point was a five. Yours was a five. Drop three hundred."

"I ain't droppin' shit! Get it how the Feds got it, bitch!" the man yelled. He was fresh home after doing twelve years. He was what you called a real live hustler back in his day. He was old school. He had heard how the streets had changed. It was a new era, a more violent one. The killers were a lot younger and more relentless.

C-Class backed out the pistol and stuck the barrel into the man's face. "Did the Feds have this?" he asked in a cocky manner.

The man laughed. "Nah. They had real guns. M16s with beams. You got a damn water pistol. Now get it out my face before I get mad."

C-Class thumbed the hammer back instead. The crowd around him backed up and slowly inched away. Prince sat on the hood of his Infinity.

The man threw his hands up. "You got it." He cautiously reached into his pocket and pulled out three crisp hundred dollar bills and dropped them the ground and stepped back. "Paid in full." He turned his back on the pistol and strolled away to the corner, turning left. The dice game jumped back off without him.

Twenty minutes later, Young Clips was still in the same position listening to the same song. Dice were still being rolled. Prime was in the back of the barbershop playing pool with C-Class. Nighttime was just starting to fall. It got dark a little earlier than usual. Young Clips noticed an old gray Honda Accord with blacked-out windows parked across the street from him. The driver door flung open and an unidentified man emerged. Young Clips studied him as he and placed his hands in the front pockets of his windbreaker jacket. He had the hood over his head and kept his eyes low as he squeezed in between the front of the 750Li and the back of Prime's Bentley parked in front of it. He headed straight into the barbershop and none of the dice players seemed to notice, but Young Clips was paying full attention. He pulled his own hoodie over his head and removed the two guns from his waist after getting out of the car. He left the door open and the engine running. He quietly crept up behind the man, who was halfway into the barbershop.

"Nice shot," C-Class complimented as Prime banked the six ball off of two rails and into the corner pocket.

"I know. I meant it to be," Prime arrogantly joked. "Two ball, side pocket," he called out his next shot, and missed. His disappointment showed as he banged the rubber at the bottom of his shooting stick into the ground. "Your shot."

C-Class smiled and hunched over the table. "Eleven ball off of the nine ball, down the tail, into the corner." His back was to the door.

Prime was looking down at the table, but something caught his eye. "Look out!"

Screams and yells could be heard in the midst of the rapid gunfire. C-Class dropped the stick and then dropped down on one knee as he slowly spun around. There he was, Young Clips, aiming two guns in his direction. He then looked down and saw someone laid face flat in his own pool of blood. The man's gun was still clutched in his hand.

Young Clips was in total shock. The pistols he held out were steaming. The fumes were intoxicating. He flashed back to the way he felt the day his radio was destroyed. He had just done the same thing with a human life, and it was easy.

Prince ran in as C-Class slowly rose to his feet, patting himself for undetected wounds. He had felt so many shots breeze by him and was thankful not to be hit. *It was a good thing Prime . . .*

"Oh shit, Prime." C-Class turned, but didn't see him. There wasn't a back exit; they were trapped off. C-Class ran around to the opposite side of the pool table and looked down. There he was, lying in his own blood.

"Prime, you all right?" C-Class asked while dropping to his knees beside him as Young Clips did the same. C-Class waved Young Clips off. "Yo! You go. Get the fuck outta here. I'll meet you back at the spot."

Young Clips reluctantly followed the order, going against his own rules to never leave a man down or behind. He hopped over spook's lifeless corpse and ran out. He jumped in the 750Li and sped off.

"Ahhh! Hell nah, I ain't a'ight. That li'l fucka shot me." Prime gasped as he held his shoulder.

"But he's the reason you're still alive though, both of us."

C-Class made his way over to the lifeless body lying on the floor. He leaned down and rolled the man over. He smiled and shook his head at the identity. He then made his way back over to Prime.

"Who the fuck was that?" Prime asked.

"The old head from the dice game earlier. Young'un was definitely on point."

"Yeah, well that's what he gets paid for," Prime stated as C-Class helped him to his feet.

The next day, Young Clips was an instant legend to the entire Alley Cats. He was already an idol. His respect spread throughout the hood; nobody told. The barber claimed the old head was outside arguing and a masked man later came in and gunned him down. It was the closest version to the truth, and all they would ever get. The strip was shut down due to the heat and the operation was moved to a new location a few blocks down. Business flowed as if it had been there for years.

Prime showed up to Young Clips's apartment with his arm in a sling. Young Clips opened the door. He didn't know whether to apologize. He remained silent while Prime spoke.

"It's all taken care of, soldier. You can come back out. By the way, C-Class owes you his life, and you owe me an arm. Consider y'all even." He tossed Young Clips the keys to his Bentley GT and then turned back around to head to his awaiting ride. "Oh, yeah." He stopped in his tracks and spun around. "It's yours," he added, before hopping in a newer and much bigger model Bentley.

Young Clips returned to the present as he reflected on the gift Prime had given him and why and how he had laid eyes on a Phantom for the first time that day. The sound of the horn of a speeding car zooming by broke his reminiscing session on how he had obtained the Bentley GT. He was parked up the street from the apartment complex Felicia was in. He wondered if it was another one of the Double Gs' spots. A half hour later, Felicia reappeared with a large duffle bag hiked over her shoulder. Young Clips watched as her wide hips sashayed to the Range Rover he had been tailing for most of the day. He got his answer as he eyed Felicia removing a gun from the duffle before tossing it in the back of her SUV.

Chapter Twenty-two

Agent McCarthy hung his head low as he scratched his scalp in frustration. He had been working diligently around the clock to get a break in the Double G investigation, but it seemed as if no matter how strong an effort he put forth, it was useless. With months of investigation and top secret intel on the organization, still they were no closer to taking down Queen Fem, Starrshma Fields, or the Double Gs than they were the first day he had announced the investigation. He grimaced at the thought. He prided himself on being a damn good investigator and he couldn't believe a group of men haters were running circles around him and every other law enforcement that did and didn't take them seriously.

"What type of freaking world do we live in?" he complained aloud. "This fuckery has to come to an end!" He pounded his fist on his metal desk. He was determined to remove what he now believed to be a thorn in his side by bringing down what he called a ruthless female gang. He came from a world where the bad guys didn't get away, and all that was connected to and associated with the Double Gs was no exception to that rule. Women or not, Agent McCarthy's mind was made up. He would dedicate all of his time and energy to this one case.

The sound of his office door hitting up against the back wall drew his attention to the unannounced body that had stormed its way inside. "Excuse me, sir!" an out-of-breath Agent Civic apologized for the intrusion.

"What is it?" Agent McCarthy wanted to know. "It better be good," he added.

"We have a name!" Agent Civic informed him.

"What do we have on her?" he asked, filled with hope as he stood up from his desk chair.

"Until now, she seemed clean as a whistle. The only reason she was even in our database is because her job requires that all employees' personal information be stored in our system," Agent Civic informed him. "Nothing serious or worth mentioning, but her name was taken down by one of the locals some years ago in connection with one of the Double G incidents. Just a random name check of innocent bystanders. I know it's a long shot, but I don't believe in any coincidences."

"That's more than we had," Agent McCarthy announced.

Agent Civic smiled like a proud son.

Agent McCarthy looked up at the ceiling. *Thank you.* He credited the tip to his Higher Power. He then drew his attention back to the agent. "So I'm assuming we have every piece of information we need on her. What about the others?"

Agent Civic shook his head from side to side. "Dead end. We'll need her to talk," he stated, knowing it wouldn't be easy.

"Shouldn't be a problem," Agent McCarthy declared with artificial optimism.

"She'll want full immunity."

"At this point she can have a senate seat in Congress. We can find a loophole later and fry her then. Let's just get her and bring her in."

"This won't be easy. No one's rolled over on them yet."

"Up until now, we've never had anyone."

"True. Good point. I'm on it."

"I'm coming along for this one. Is she at work now?"

"Yup! Her boss has been informed to keep here there without suspicion."

"Good work. Where'd they get the trucks?"

"The plates were switched around. Not exactly a felony."

"Figures."

"Any luck with your mole?"

"Mole?" Agent McCarthy asked with sarcasm.

"I set myself up for that one."

"Nice try, kid." Agent McCarthy smiled at Agent Civic's wit. It had become an office discussion as to his alleged plant in the Double G organization. Everyone wanted to know whether it was true and if so they wanted to know who was it and how he had managed to pull it off. That was the furthest thing from Agent McCarthy's mind though. He was more focused on the lead they had just received. *I promise to make this one count.* He peered up one more time, as he snatched his jacket from behind his desk seat and made a beeline toward his office doorway.

Chapter Twenty-three

After finally making it home, Starr expected to fall into a deep sleep the moment her head hit the pillow. Instead, she tossed and turned until she found a comfortable position and drifted off. Ever since she had left Diamond's place and climbed into her own bed, she had been restless. Whenever she got like that, she always traveled back in time. She would be so comatose that it was as if she were watching a movie starring herself when she slept that hard. Accounts of her childhood continued to invade her thoughts. It was common for the thoughts to appear without notice. It had been a minute since she had taken a trip down memory lane, but now images of her as a child jumped around in her mind. Much of her young childhood was a blur. Many times, her dreams would turn into nightmares, causing her to wake up in a cold sweat.

They usually started out with the same scene: her mother giving birth to her at the young age of thirteen or her mother smiling down at her and cradling her like a doll baby in a lavender and white bedroom full of stuffed animals and toys. The image would soon transform into her mother's smile turning to a frown, while she still cradled her in the same manner. Only this time, tears streamed down her face and the lively room filled with stuffed animals and toys were replaced with an alleyway, trash bags, rats, and stray cats. For the first four years of Starr's life, she and her mother were homeless.

Images of her mother wrapping her up in filthy blankets and covering her with garbage bags played in Starr's head. *"This is the only way I can keep you safe and warm while Mommy's out getting us something to eat,"* Starr remembered her mother telling her. She devoured a sandwich while she listened to every word her mother expressed to her. "Never trust any man. Ever!" was stressed every day to her and embedded in Starr's young mind. Images of the wounds, scars, and contusions her mother revealed to her that were supposedly caused by a man every time she went out in search of food to keep her and Starr alive were the evidence she offered as the reason why her daughter should stay away from men.

The scene changed to when Starr reached age five. The image of her mother running down the alley screaming her name at the top of her lungs appeared. She could still see the pale white figure trailing behind her mother. The image switched to Starr about to come from behind the Dumpster until she heard the loud bang. She peered around the metal container and witnessed her mother laid flat on her stomach. She was wide-eyed, with a horrific look on her face, while the man who gave chase kneeled over her with what appeared to be a gun in his hand. She reflected on how she watched as he retrieved a brown leather wallet from her mother. Starr assumed it belonged to him. The image of Starr running out of the alleyway she had once known as home skipped through her mind. It immediately skipped to the moment she ran headfirst into a short, plump woman with blond hair and blue eyes and a warm and inviting smile plastered across her face.

Mary Reynolds adored children but couldn't bear her own. She was enchanted by a young Starr and took her home with her. Starr remembered it was where she had gotten her nickname. It was Mary who had always referred to her as her shining Starr. Starr remembered how her fake mother, as she thought of her, her husband Harry was not fond on her bringing Starr home.

Eventually he warmed up to having a child around. Starr's life skipped to nine and a half years later. One day her fake mother went off to work and never came back. Starr had overheard Harry Reynolds saying she had gotten into a terrible highway accident after taking a detour to get a few things for Starr's upcoming thirteenth birthday party. After a full year and a half, things began to take a drastic change for the worse. Starr flashed to the time when her fake father began drinking very heavily.

Starr's life jumped to when she was fifteen and her body began to rapidly develop. She noticed all of her young curves had started to fill out. Her fake father had also started to notice, she recalled.

Starr's life skipped as she slipped into a mental trip down memory lane to one evening when she had explored herself in the shower. *The water was steaming hot, just how Starr liked it. She let it beat down on her back as she lathered up her flawless adolescent body. Every now and then, a cool draft would slip through, causing her nipples to harden. She gently stroked the body sponge across each one as she closed her eyes, and lightly pressed her top row of teeth into the middle of her bottom lip. She savored every moment of the sensation and self-inflicted arousal.*

Her senses heightened to a supreme level. Before she knew it, her finger slipped in between her legs. Her subconscious couldn't traverse the fiery temptation. She began manually manipulating her clitoris into an orgasmic pulse, riding the rhythm into shock waves of explosive ecstasy. This was a ritual that she had also found out was part of becoming a woman. It was an accident at first. It eventually became her secret.

She quietly began to moan as her knees weakened. She cocked her head back and let the hot water beat down across her forehead, and into her long hair as she shut her eyes tighter, bringing her closer to an orgasm. Starr remembered the particular orgasm feeling different than normal. A draft blanketed her body for a brief second and then disappeared. It seemed to be just the extra stimulation she needed. Her moans turned into rapid, short breaths, and a silent, steady moan as her body began to tremble. The release had occurred, loosening every muscle in her entire body, draining her of all energy.

After the final deep exhalation, Starr opened her eyes. Her vision was still blurry. She reached up for her towel, gripping nothing but air. It was gone. Assuming it had dropped, she quickly pulled back the sliding shower glass, only to see Harry standing there staring at her complete nakedness. Naturally, her first reaction was to scream. She was not only startled, but embarrassed. Embarrassment turned to fear. Harry didn't budge. Starr could tell he was still highly intoxicated and probably had staggered in to urinate when he stumbled on to her erotic peep show.

Starr tried to shut the glass shower door, but he caught it with his right hand and slid it back open. Starr's eyes widened in horror. The image of Harry stepping forward, forcing himself into the shower dominated Starr's nightmare. As hard as she tried, she couldn't get past him. He was too strong for her. He blanketed her body with his own, and trapped her against the shower wall. He kissed on her neck as she squirmed, trying to free herself. She began to get violent. She kicked, scratched, and screamed. Nothing worked. He was unfazed.

Harry picked Starr up and threw her over his shoulder, carrying her to her room, and dropped her onto the bed. He tried to climb on top of her, but as he did, he landed directly on a flying knee right into his groin. A sharp pain went straight to his gut as he buckled. He rolled off of her and the bed, falling onto the carpeted floor. He began throwing up on impact.

Starr wasted no time hopping up and out of the bed. She grabbed her robe to cover her body and tried to run past him in an attempt to make it out of the house. Harry reached out, grabbed her by the ankle, and tripped her on her face, spraining her right hand. They were both on the floor. Harry got himself together and pulled her into his chest. She tried to resist but was overpowered.

Once Harry got her into his arms, he just held on to her until his breathing returned normal. Starr could tell that he had calmed down, but still she tried to break free every chance she got. An image of Harry crying and hugging her even tighter appeared.

She began to feel kisses on her neck again. She was surprised, confused, afraid but, strangest of all, understanding. She shut her eyes tight as her own tears escaped, and braced herself for whatever was about to happen. The scene jumped to Starr showering for a second time. That night she made a promise that she would never allow another man to touch her in any form. When she returned to her room, she stuffed as many of her belongings as could fit into a duffle and snuck out of her home undetected.

Her painful journey back in time was interrupted by the sound of her text message ring tone on her phone blaring in the air. She recognized the number and opened up the message. Judging by the text, she immediately noticed the texter was not the owner of the phone.

Who is this? Starr rapidly texted back, thinking the worst.

She sat up as the girl introduced herself via text and ran down the details of the nature of her call and how she came to have the phone. Starr thanked her for the information and told her someone would be there momentarily to retrieve the phone. She scrolled through her contacts and dialed out. Diamond answered on the first ring.

"We have a situation," Starr announced before relaying the story that was just told to her.

Chapter Twenty-four

The day had been going smoothly just like any other day for Careese Pearson at her Bank of America job. She had been a bank teller for six years strong now. She was still shocked and surprised by her supervisor's offer. She wondered if she should take those extra hours her boss had just offered her. *With a raise? Why not?* she thought. Up until today, they weren't even getting along. Maybe he had finally come around and noticed how good a worker she was. She kept her breaks brief. She was out of the way and completely off the radar, just like she had always been instructed to be. Maintaining a legit high-end job was a golden rule of the Double G. Every day she awoke, she made sure she protected both her job and her affiliation with the organization she had been a part of for the past five years, thanks to her recruiter, Diamond.

Careese's thoughts were interrupted by the sudden burst into the bank. A sense of panic jolted her body at the thought of a bank robbery.

That thought was immediately excused when she noticed the bold letters on the back of the intruders' jackets. Federal agents spilled into the bank one after the other. Like all the other workers, she wondered what was going on. She didn't have to wonder too long. She noticed the agents seemed to be headed in her direction.

Agent McCarthy was the first to reach her. "Careese Pearson? We need you to come with us," he announced with authority.

Careese's heart dropped into her plus-sized panties. She feared the worst and was right. She just wondered what they knew.

Two agents wasted no time. "Sorry, ma'am," the two agents sang in unison as they grabbed hold of each of her arms and gently placed them behind her back. She dropped her head low in embarrassment as she was escorted out of the bank by the agents. They were so focused on her that they had never noticed the teller who was working next to her quickly swipe up her cell phone and fade into the background.

Since the two had become close she had learned a lot about Careese Pearson, which was why she didn't object when her friend instructed her months ago to contact someone for her if anything was to ever happen to her.

Olivia Brown knew this warranted that something she had referred to. She looked around nervously. While they conducted their arrest and search of Careese's station, Olivia slipped into a blind spot.

She typed in the four-digit pass code she had been given and told to remember. Once it was open, she pulled up the contact and began texting away. As all of the agents were making their way out of the bank, with her friend in cuffs, she awaited an acknowledging response. She nervously glanced from the agents back down to the phone. She used her thumb to scroll through the phone until the only programmed number stored in it that belonged to her only friend popped up.

Meanwhile, downtown in the old Las Vegas area, the Black Yukon Denali sped away, cutting through traffic. It pulled up to the back of this huge, tinted-glass building with assorted federal vehicles parked around it. The agent who was driving flashed his badge at the camera and waved. The gate rolled up and the Yukon drove through the dark underground tunnel. It went the entire length and came into a large lit area. There was nothing else there but an elevator.

The agents got out and looked up at the overhead camera. Moments later, the metal gate opened. They escorted Careese out of the SUV and into the elevator.

Up until that point, she hadn't said a word and neither had the agents. They just mean mugged her and handled her roughly. She masked her nervousness with a sarcastic smirk at every agent who looked at her with blatant disgust, showing that the feeling was mutual.

The elevator stopped on the seventh floor. She was steered down a long, carpeted walkway. There were agents everywhere trying to act casual, but cutting their eyes at her as they bounced around from office cube to office cube. Phones rang, fax machines beeped, and the stench of stale coffee was in the air. At the end of the hall was a large white door, which also had a camera facing down at them. Someone behind the scenes had to press buttons all day. *Damn. They don't even trust their own,* she thought. They stepped through and into a narrow hallway with six doors on each side. She was placed in the second room on the right.

Agent McCarthy yanked her by her elbow and sat her at the wood grain table. "Have a seat," he ordered.

She looked the opposite way of him with full attitude, but did as she was told. Agent McCarthy walked around her. He leaned in over her shoulder from behind her, resting the palm of his left hand on the table, and he whispered into her ear, "We're going to put you and the rest of them away for life." He then rose back up and exited the room.

Careese jumped from the slamming sound the metal door made. She was left in the cold room by herself. But not really alone, she knew. There was a two-way mirror on both full-length walls, one in front of her and one in back. There was a built-in audio recorder that sat in the center of the table where many confessions and helpful information had been exchanged at the expense of the lives of others.

She looked around to study the rest of the room. There was a camera above the door, pointing down at her. The carpeted floor was gray and there were no windows.

All track of time was lost. When left alone and under pressure, minutes felt like hours. But Careese did her best to maintain her composure, despite her current predicament. She knew it was in her best interest to keep cool. She had been groomed and prepped for situations such as the one she was in. She was well aware that Agent McCarthy was trying to intimidate her.

But she knew there was nothing he could do or say worse than what would happen to her if she did open her mouth about anything.

"I'd like to call my attorney," she exercised her rights. She wanted Agent McCarthy to know she wasn't a pushover. She knew he was listening and watching.

To no surprise to her, the room's door flew open and Agent McCarthy reemerged. He walked around to where she had a full view of him. He now stood directly in front of her, with only the table between them. He placed both fists on the wooden tabletop and leaned in until they were face to face. "You sure about that?" A shit-eating grin appeared across his face.

He was so close she could smell his lunch and cheap aftershave. The foul stench tickled her nose. She couldn't believe he sported the old-school fragrance she had recognized. She didn't think men wore Brute 22 anymore.

"Yes, I'm sure." She rolled her eyes as she answered.

Agent McCarthy raised his fists from the table. "Okay, suit yourself." He sighed. "Ms. Careese Lavern Pearson, you are under arrest for conspiracy to operate under the management of organized crime. You have the right to remain silent." Agent McCarthy informed her of the offenses she was being charged with then began reading her Miranda rights.

He smiled on the inside as he observed Careese Pearson's demeanor change from stoic to shocked.

Chapter Twenty-five

Her heels were heard echoing as they tapped the hard marble floor when she cleared through the revolving doors. All attention was drawn to her as she dominantly strutted by a circle of stars: the Federal Bureau logo. She confidently approached the front desk and set her Armani Exchange briefcase on top of the high wood grain horseshoe-shaped countertop. She looked down at the middle-age officer who was sitting low in the front of a brass desk, lamp shining down on the logbook. A younger officer was standing at full attention in front of the metal detector checking her out, admiring her beauty. He noticed how her deep, dark skin glowed, despite no sunlight or any form of bright lighting being in the building.

Standing at an even six feet, naturally, she was tall for a woman, but the heels embellished her height even more. Her jet-black long, thick hair was pulled back into a tight ponytail revealing the natural slant of her eyes. The click-clack sound made by her six-inch heels resembled that of a prize-winning thoroughbred's trot. Her thin platinum Cartier French frames sat at the end of the bridge of her nose just below her high cheekbones. Occasionally she would push them back up with her manicured pointer finger to prevent them from slipping off of her face as she strutted through the precinct building. Her diamond earrings sparkled along with her thin platinum chain with a single diamond pendant. Her breasts protruded at the top of her blouse, allowing the pendant to lie just above her cleavage. It rose up with each step she took. Her silk blouse was white, covered by a dark gray blazer that matched the bottom half of her two-piece skirt suit. Anyone who trailed behind her would have perfect access to the perfect heart-shaped, plump ass that filled up her skirt. She had hips for days and her long, vibrant legs were massive. Her ass poked out and the under cuff revealed the slight imprint of her Elle Macpherson boy shorts.

As the young officer eyed her from head to toe, he saw that her right leg sported an expensive-looking diamond anklet that sat over the strap of her Manolo Blahniks stilettos. Her bright red lipstick parted to reveal her perfect teeth as she smiled at the younger deputy before looking back down and handing the front desk officer her ID and business credentials. He studied both and then looked back up at her with a smile before entering her into the logbook.

"You want to go right up to the seventh floor," he stated. "He'll escort you to the elevator, ma'am," he added as he pointed over to the standing officer who was pleased to perform his duty.

"Thank you," she replied while pulling her briefcase down to her side. She adjusted her frames as she strolled through the walk-through metal detector.

The younger officer was really hoping the alarm would ring off until she would have to be forced to strip naked.

As she cleared it she spread her arms wide for him to scan her with the hand device. *Damn Feds don't trust oxygen,* she thought as she passed him her briefcase.

He set it on an X-ray machine and watched the screen as it went through. He then escorted her to the elevator. "Have a nice day." He politely bowed, tipping his hat.

"I always do," she retorted as the elevator doors shut him out and her in. *And this is my favorite part of it,* she continued to herself, smiling. She then turned to the elevator officer.

"Seventh floor, please," she declared, turning on her full attitude. The curtain had just been raised. The show was on. Diamond stared at the numbers as the elevator climbed upward. She put her game face on as the elevator's dial lit up on the number seven.

Just a few doors up the hallway, "That's bullshit!" were the words Careese Pearson spewed and Agent Donahue walked in on as he entered the interrogation room.

Agent Donahue was a middle-aged white agent who had been in the Bureau for as long as Tom McCarthy. McCarthy's presence was scary and uninviting. He was huge with broad shoulders. His jaw line structure was frightening. His upright posture was still as strong as it was in his college football days. His wide frame left no extra space in his suit. His voice was convicting. Donahue was the exact opposite. He was smooth, friendly, diplomatic, and deceivingly frail. Above all, he was extremely smart.

"No, sweetheart! This is all real," Agent McCarthy retorted. "We have evidence proving that you are in fact a part of the Double G organization," he bellowed. "And that you also helped murder two young, innocent agents! That's capital punishment! Lethal injection!"

He laid it on thick, wondering if he had gone overboard with his interrogation tactic. He was in a zone though. "What do you think, Agent Donahue?" he aggressively called out, noticing the agent's sudden presence. He then drew his attention back to Careese, whose eyes were now wider than they were previously.

Agent Donahue's tone was soft. "No, no, Agent McCarthy. She did no such thing. They manipulated her. It's not her fault. They set her up to take the fall. She was clearly just caught up with the wrong people. Unfortunately, they're hanging her out to dry," he calmly explained with his face in her opposite ear.

"To dry?" Agent McCarthy released a sarcastic laugh. "No. More like to burn!" he yelled into her other ear, shaking her up. "Look at the pictures!" he demanded, forcing her to view the autopsy photos of Agents Mullin and Craven, and the other ones from the crime scene. "They got off a lot easier than you will. You're going to be alive to suffer your death!" he yelled, sending chills through her.

"No, she won't," Donahue calmly intervened. "She's here to help us. She doesn't like what happened to those poor young agents any more than we do. We have her full cooperation from here on out. Don't we, Ms. Pearson?" he asked, looking into her eyes. Her face was sandwiched between them both as she looked down at the brutal pictures spread all over the table.

Careese didn't know what to do or say. They were coming at her so hard, left and right. She couldn't escape the balanced attack of their voices. They were in her head, thinking for her. They barely even asked her questions. She started to get scared. *Lethal injections? Life? Am I ready for that? But I made a vow,* she reasoned. *Double Gs for life,* chimed in her head. Her options were not good. Her heart rate rose as she began to panic. It was getting hot. No, the air conditioner was on full blast, she remembered. It was freezing. *Well, it was a minute ago. What do I do? Does anyone even know I'm here? I'm all by myself. They're going to fry me. No. I didn't do anything. Did I?* Her mind was all over the place. She tried to shake it off. They were fucking with her, she knew. Her thoughts were interrupted.

"Listen." Donahue set his attention on Careese and then looked over at McCarthy. "Where's your hospitality? Get the lady some coffee while I speak to her in private, will you?" he asked in a delicate tone.

"All right. But I'll be right back. And when I return, she's mine!" he announced before he exited.

Careese shook as the door slammed shut behind Agent McCarthy. As Donahue took a seat directly across from her and held her trembling hands, her palms were so cold, yet sweaty. Her eyes seemed distant. They had her. It was time for the kill.

Agent McCarthy walked into the next room, loosened up his tie, and smiled at the other three agents who were monitoring it all from behind the two-way mirror. "I give her five minutes. We'll have all the information we need," he gloated as they shook their heads agreeing, enjoying the show. He watched like a proud parent as Agent Donahue played good cop.

"Listen. What I want from you is to explain it to me. Just me. I know you didn't hurt anyone. But the reality of it is that two agents were killed. And you didn't do it. But accessory is like pulling the trigger yourself. Especially when you're the only person we have for this to fall on. Meanwhile, whoever protecting you left you for dead. That's just the reality of it. The fact remaining is that we're the only people who can help you now. Well, I am. Agent McCarthy would rather destroy you," Agent Donahue informed her. "He and those murdered agents were real close," he added.

"But me, I just want justice. Making you the fall guy isn't justice." His tone became more empathetic. "It's vengeance. I don't want vengeance. I just want the truth. Once I have that, I won't even need you any longer; you'd be free to go. Back to your job at the bank. No one will even know you were here. We'll make it seem like we thought you may have been stealing from the bank. A false indictment to show people usually works. I promise I will go the distance for you. But first," he said, and pushed the pen and paper in her direction, "I need to know exactly what happened two nights ago. And you're free to go."

Careese looked down at the pen and paper. Its letterhead read, CONFIDENTIAL CONFESSION/ CLASSIFIED. She stared at the photos of the murdered agents scattered across the table. And then she looked back at the paper, back at the pictures, and then at the pen. With broken reluctance, she slowly reached for it. Her hand jerked back as the door burst open.

"Get the hell away from my client!" Diamond yelled out like a female lioness protecting her young as she slammed her briefcase down on the table and scooped up the group of pictures along with the statement forms and the pen in front of Careese. "I don't believe any of this concerns her, so I'd advise you to end your line of questioning.

Now!" she sternly stated. She smacked him in the chest with the items that were on the table when she first entered the interrogation room.

"What're you doin' here?" Completely caught by surprise, Agent Donahue fumbled to catch the items just in time before they hit the floor. Diamond's arrogance transformed him from the once good cop he was pretending to be to Careese Pearson back to his normal asshole self. His friendliness was gone. "What does this have to do with you?" he followed up with.

"I was just about to ask you the same thing. But not before I asked why the hell my hard-working, tax-paying, law-abiding citizen of a client is being held under false pretenses," Diamond retorted. She knew he couldn't possibly know who she really was. No one outside of their organization really did.

Agent McCarthy abruptly burst in. He had the look of a defeated man as Diamond continued, "She isn't under arrest. Why was she detained?" She wasted no time cutting into Agent McCarthy. "She's no criminal. And unless you come up with proof of otherwise, I advise y'all to stay as far away from her as possible in the same state, unless you want to be downgraded to traffic cops. I've already spoken to your superiors.

They're not pleased. I've also spoken to the magistrate judge who claimed to have no knowledge of a warrant being sought for the detention of my client. The truth is y'all never gave her the opportunity to cooperate. Y'all embarrassed her at her job, which she might not even have any longer. All y'all had to do was call her, which still would've been a dead end. She doesn't know anything. Nor has she done anything. But you, gentlemen, have done something. You publicly embarrassed and humiliated my client at her workplace. In addition to that, I'm sure that her job is in jeopardy, if they haven't already filed for immediate termination. So, unless you plan on falsely charging her with something, this meeting is over."

Diamond politely stated, "Oh, and y 'all can expect to hear from my firm again, but on liability charges this time. Y'all have a good day, gentlemen," she ended as she unleashed verbal assault all in one breath.

She then snatched Careese up by her arm and pulled her out of the door, before Agent McCarthy or Donahue had a chance to rebut her claims and accusations. Just as she reached the door with Careese in tow, she turned and faced Agent McCarthy.

"Oh, and give Linda my love. She knows me." Diamond shot Agent McCarthy a wink and a smile then stormed off leaving with the Federal Bureau of Investigation's possibly best lead on their organization. The only one they'd had.

An egg could've been fried on Agent McCarthy's face he was so heated. He stood there watching the arrogant attorney sashay out of the building. His pressure went from zero to one hundred, not only because she had walked away with who he believed to be his star potential witness, but because of the mention of his wife's name. He made a mental note to ask her about the cocky plus-sized female attorney working for who he believed to be the Double Gs.

"Can she do that?" Agent Donahue asked McCarthy as the two men stood there dumbfounded.

"She just did," McCarthy replied dryly. "It was a long shot." He shrugged his shoulders and shook his head. "And we were this close to a damn confession." He illustrated with his two fingers. "It would've been all we needed." He was sure he had gotten Careese Pearson on the ropes and, up until the unexpected presence of her attorney, Agent Donahue was doing a great job wrapping things up. He sucked his teeth and cursed himself for not closing on the interrogation personally. He had gotten too excited and was now paying for it. Had he stayed focused on the main objective he wouldn't have let up on the Double Gs' puppet until he got a signed confession. That was now a distant memory. McCarthy chalked this incident up as a loss for the home team.

"So what now?" Agent Donahue asked. He was still in shock behind Diamond walking in and whisking out a potential key witness and informant against the female organization he too had now taken seriously.

"Good question." McCarthy grimaced. "Back to square one." He sucked his teeth and pounded his right fist into his left palm. "Dammit!" he then abruptly let out as he smacked both palms down on the hardwood table.

"After you." Diamond let Careese out of the elevator before she herself exited. The nervous look on Careese's face did not go unnoticed. But Diamond paid her facial expression and fidgety demeanor no mind. No words were exchanged the whole ride down from the seventh floor, where Careese was just being detained. She walked back past the metal detector and back out of the revolving door through which she had entered, as Careese trailed behind. Neither of them uttered a word to the other until they were safely enclosed in Diamond's Maserati.

Diamond pulled out her cell phone. "Yeah, I got her," Diamond informed Starr. Seconds later she ended the call.

"Thank you, girl. That was too much." Careese gasped as soon as Diamond hung up.

"What were you thinkin'?" Diamond snapped. "You should know better than to let them trap you off without me present. Or any lawyer for that matter! I need to know everything you told them or I won't be able to defend you."

Careese began to play the tape back for Diamond from the time the agents swarmed the bank up until the time she had entered the interrogation room and whisked her up out of there. Diamond was sure she had seen Careese ready to reach for the pen and pad the agent had placed in front of her. Everyone in that room knew she had intervened just in time, including Careese. Diamond listened carefully to her and made a mental note to inform Starr about what she had witnessed.

Chapter Twenty-six

Another night of waking up in a cold sweat almost drove him insane. The nightmares seemed to get worse. Was it his conscience? For the most part, the guilt was a burden. The nightmare was a constant punishment, a brutal one. The things he and his partner were forced to do: the murders, the violence, and the stealing from the evidence room. So many things compiled as a whole, thought Officer Douglass. It was stacked against him, enough to put him away for life, and he couldn't take it any longer. He thought he could handle it, thought it was over, but it wasn't. And he was a fool for believing it ever would be.

Weeks had passed since, according to Blake, they had carried out the last job. So when his partner and friend called him with a sob story about one more job being the official last one, his mind was made up. There was no way he could see himself putting everything from his career to freedom on the line again. By the grace of God he believed he had escaped and now he was not willing to step back into the lion's den. His only hope was that he'd somehow receive leniency for the information he planned to provide.

It's perfect timing. With the fresh death of two federal agents, they will worship me for being able to help. I'll be a hero who is looked at as a victim who finally willed himself to get strong enough to do the right thing, he convinced himself. It was a hell of a risk, but so was everything else he was being forced to do against his will. He knew by coming clean it meant throwing his partner under the bus as well. He was torn between regret and fear, but he felt there was no way of getting around it. A small price to pay for peace of mind and a good night's rest, Douglass weighed it up as. He took a deep breath and exhaled. He then rapped his knuckles on the pane glass of his superior officer's door.

The words, "Come in," caused his heart rate to quicken. Douglass slowly turned the door knob and entered the office.

"What is it, Douglass?" Chief Andrews looked up over his reading glasses. He was preoccupied reading over the reports due before the day was out, concerning a 211 that turned into a 187.

"Sir, may I sit?" Douglass's voice cracked as he spoke.

"Make it fast." Chief Andrews extended his hand to the wooden chair in front of him. "I really got my hands full with this gay bike group crap," he added.

There was a brief pause. "That's kind of why I'm here, sir." The nervousness could be detected in his tone.

Chief Andrews dropped his pen down onto the papers he had been sifting through. He leaned back in his desk chair and clasped his hands together. "You have information on the Double G case?"

Officer Douglass bit the inside of his gum. "I have more than information on the Double Gs, sir."

Chief Andrews leaned forward with a peculiar look on his face. Something in Officer Douglass's tone raised an eyebrow. "Do I need to pull out the tape recorder, Douglass?"

Officer Douglass nodded his head and took another deep breath. Chief Andrews went into his desk drawer. Seconds later, he was spilling his guts. Twenty-five minutes later Chief Andrews pressed stop on the tape recorder.

"Are you sure you want to go through with this?" Chief Andrews asked Douglass after hearing the chilling confession. He was still trying to take it all in. Never in a million years would he have thought Douglass and Blake to be crooked cops. Although he partially understood the circumstances, based on what Douglass had revealed, there was no excuse in the chief's eyes when it came to not upholding the law. The blinds in his office were drawn low. The chief had lowered them once Officer Douglass informed him of the nature of his visit to his office.

Douglass was now in tears. He didn't hold back one single detail. He let it all be known exactly the way he remembered it. He painted vivid pictures so that he would be safe from his leverage coming back to haunt him. After being on that side of the law for so long, he knew exactly how rolling over on somebody worked. Whatever you left out, the other person would bring up and make it look like other stuff was being held back. He left his partner with no tuck cards of his own. He would be awarded extreme leniency and Officer Blake would fry. Fry for dragging him into this mess. When they were just skimming money from raids and planting the same drugs they had just arrested somebody else for on another charge, it was cool. The partying with hookers was one thing, but to become a professional hit man on call who wasn't even paid, that was something different. He didn't care what they had on Blake or what Blake had on him. It was all out in the open now. The truth would set him free, full immunity.

Chief Andrews had been on the force sixteen years. He hadn't been shocked by much. But everything he heard in the past few hours was terrifying. It was then that he understood why Agent McCarthy was so passionate about this specific case. These women were terrorists. And they had cells everywhere. Even on the inside. Their power couldn't be second-guessed. There was only one thing to do now.

Chief Andrews stared Office Douglass in the eyes in silence. Office Douglass couldn't stop moving his trembling body the entire time he was confessing. "You know this is out of my hands. I have to turn you over to a good friend of mine who will protect you; well, until it blows over. Where's Officer Blake now?"

Officer Douglass looked at his watch. "Our shift starts in a half. He should be here in ten; he's always early."

"Well, I'm going to make the call now. What I need you to do is stall him," the chief instructed Officer Douglass.

"So what will happen with me?"

"Truthfully, you'll both be arrested on the spot. But that's just to make it look good. And then you'll be separated. We'll have his side of the story and we'll check into a few things. If they match up, we'll push for full immunity, along with the witness protection program, a new identity for you, your wife, and your daughter."

Just being reminded of his family made Officer Douglass wonder if he was doing the right thing. It was so risky. Either way they were in jeopardy. Surely this would be the only thing to keep them safe. By the time anyone figured out what was going on, they would be long gone. *Maybe Toronto.*

"So what now?" Officer Douglass asked.

"I'll make the call," Chief Andrews stated.

While picking up the phone and holding it between his ear and shoulder to keep his hands free, he nodded his head toward the entrance of his office door. "You go stall Blake," he instructed Douglass before placing his call.

Chapter Twenty-seven

When one door slams in your face another one opens. At least Agent McCarthy believed so. He was ecstatic to come right back up on such a promising lead after just losing Careese Pearson. Still it saddened him to hear of such corruption within the law enforcement department. It never ended, he thought. The scale of justice had been tipped and the government was losing.

"All right, just keep them there. I can't make any solid promises, Andrews, but I'm going to at least try to get him immunity, cocksucking son of a bitch!" he chimed. "Only if he leads to a conviction," he added. "And it ain't gonna be easy. But I swear if even one word of his confession is false, I'll have his corpse remanded to a prison cell after he dies. I'm sending my men." He ended, "Oh, and Chief?"

"Yes?"

"Thanks. I owe you."

"No, you don't. We're on the same side, remember?"

Agent McCarthy flashed a reserved grin. The chief's words were comforting. It had been hard for him lately. He didn't know who was who. Only situations like this swayed his evaluations. "That's what I like to hear," he replied. "I'm sending two of my best men and a small team to help them out. There are not many others I can trust. Those guys are still so fucked up over Mullin's and Craven's deaths that they are doing everything they can to help."

"So am I," Chief Andrews solidified.

They both hung up. Agent McCarthy jumped up from his desk smiling as he regained all hope stronger than before. There was no more credible witness than a cop. All they needed was any one piece of tangible evidence to substantiate it all and the FBI could start raining down indictments so hard, just to not be associated with the Double Gs a lesbian would turn straight until it was all over.

Agent McCarthy swerved around his desk while fixing his tie. His eyes widened as his office door swung open hard. He stared up at one of the meanest faces he had ever seen. He wondered to what he owed the pleasure of his superior paying him a visit. Agent McCarthy rose to greet Agent Mobley.

"Have a seat, Tom," Mobley demanded more than suggested.

"I'm on a big lead. Give me like fi—"

"Now!" Agent Mobley declared, cutting him short of his words.

McCarthy turned and sat back down at his desk. "Wassup?" He tossed his hands behind his head in frustration.

"I'm removing you from this case."

Agent McCarthy nearly fell out of his chair. He couldn't believe his ears. "What? Like hell you are!" he cried out loud. "I just got the biggest freaking break ever!"

"I don't give a goddamn!" Agent Mobley interjected. "You fucked up, Tom. With the Pearson girl when you unlawfully detained her." He sarcastically added, "Not to mention the tail leading to the death of two of our agents."

The words stung Agent McCarthy's heart and ego like a pack of killer bees.

"Now, you will hand over your so-called leads and files over to Agent Reddick and brief him. You've put the whole Bureau in jeopardy of one of the biggest lawsuits we've ever been up against. You were too close to the agents who were murdered. It's a conflict and has affected your judgment." His superior concluded, "Look at you, Tom. You haven't been sleeping in weeks."

Agent McCarthy looked at Agent Mobley with a questionable eye. He tried to speak, but was stopped by the palm of Agent Mobley's hand. "I've said all I have to say about the matter. There's nothing else left to discuss. I'm doing this for your own good, but even more for this department. This Diamond Morgan hasn't lost a federal case yet. She's the best. Ask your wife about her; Linda will tell you that as long as she's been the best US attorney for the eastern district, Ms. Morgan is the only one who haunts her. No one wants to fight a civil suit. Blame yourself. You should've come to me first. I got people to answer to too, you know. Expect to be relieved by Agent Reddick shortly. I'll have him meet you in the situation room." With that said Ronald Mobley shut the door behind him.

This has to be some fucking nightmare. Please wake me, Agent McCarthy said to himself. *Agent Reddick?* he questioned in his mind. "Fuck!" he screamed. Then all in one motion, he slammed both palms of his hands down on the desk and swiped all of the files off it like a madman. Paper flew everywhere.

After all the goddamn work I've done! They're going to pull me? He still couldn't believe it. *Fucking politics.* It was officially out of his hands now. But he wasn't going to let that stop him.

As far as he was concerned, the city would be a better place without the organization. He had done all in his power to take them down. But he knew he had to do more if he wanted Starrshma Fields or the rest of Double G to crumble. If they got away without proper prosecution, it would be his colleagues' fault. He couldn't let that happen. McCarthy was beyond pissed at their inability to see how dangerous the Double Gs were. But if nobody else was going to fight to rid the streets of Las Vegas of them, Agent McCarthy was determined to. *I may have lost the battle, but I refuse to lose the war,* he told himself as he pulled out the spare phone.

Chapter Twenty-eight

"What?" Monica hysterically whispered into the phone, still in disbelief of what she was hearing. For months she had been getting deeper and deeper within the organization. Deeper than any other she had ever heard about. The last thing she wanted to hear was that there was division within the Bureau. "So what do I do now?" she asked in search of any responsible answer. She wasn't sure whether McCarthy was trying to pull the plug on the operation.

There's no way I'm going to accept being pulled out, she concluded. Not when she had come this far. If she gave up now, everything she had put her life on the line for would have been done for nothing. "You know how much this means to me," she reminded him. "If I have to go rogue, I will," she threatened. Her tone was more aggressive than her normal mild one.

"Just relax," Agent McCarthy tried to calm her. "No one's pulling you out. That's not what

I'm saying." He clarified, "There's just a few kinks that need to be ironed out. Until then, you just stay in deep cover. You will still report to no one but me. If anyone ever contacts you from the agency, it's when you've been made, don't trust them. I have your real identity. I'm the only one. I'm the only person who can give it back to you when this is over. So try not to get caught by law enforcement. But still do whatever it is you have to do to get to the top. God forbid if anything does happen. I'll be the first one on the scene."

"But what if something happens to you first?" she asked.

That was something he had never thought about and there was no real answer. "For both of our sakes, let just hope it doesn't." That was all he could conjure up for reassurance.

"I can't believe this, Tom. Something's not right about this." She sighed.

"Tell me about it. But, don't worry, I'm all over it. Fuck what Mobley or anybody else says."

"I'm glad to hear you say that, because I'm getting so close. I can feel it." She felt a little better hearing Agent McCarthy's words. "Speaking of which . . ." She paused. It pained her just thinking about it. "I'm not sure if it's connected or a coincidence, but the Washington girl who goes by the name Bubbles was telling me a story that's similar to my brother's case. Before she could finish, she was interrupted by one of the other members."

"So, what do you have?" Agent McCarthy asked.

"I need you to look up murders during the time of my brother's. See if any of them owned a BMW, model preferably a 325i."

"I'm sure you're going to tell me why," he chimed.

Monica thought she had heard something. She looked behind her and then whispered into the phone, "I'll be in touch."

"Be safe," Agent McCarthy stated.

His words went unheard. She had already disconnected the call.

Chapter Twenty-nine

The silver Phantom pulled up in front of Treasures as Freeze and Esco sat in the back finishing up a game of *NBA Live*. Tonight's wager was five grand. Both men thumbed the controllers vigorously while hundreds of partygoers on the line waited to get in. The scenery quickly shifted in a blink of an eye. First two motorcycles shot down the street without warning as human and vehicle traffic quickly scattered to clear the way just in time. The two matching pink and black R6s traveled at top speed and then in an instant they simultaneously hit their front brakes performing tricks as their back wheels lifted high up while their front wheels balanced the bikes, skidding down the length of the street, stopping and dropping the back wheels back down as they paused in between both clubs. The infamous roars of engines could be heard echoing in the air. Freeze dropped the PlayStation remote controller on the floor and stepped out of the Phantom. He stood in the streets with his arms folded, leaning against the vehicle. Numerous bikes with passengers on the back shot past him performing all sorts of tricks and stunts. Esco let himself out of the Phantom as well and also spilled into the streets and pulled up next to his partner in crime.

The two stretch Escalades slowly pulled up between both clubs as people cheered. They stopped in front of the Phantom. It was the closest Freeze had ever been to Starr. He watched as the driver stepped out and walked around the back and helped them step down. Starr purposely let herself out on Freeze's side. She revealed a devious grin as she cut her eyes at him that only Freeze caught. His face twisted up and turned to stone. Bubbles got out on the other side and the doors from the second Escalade opened wide. Both Freeze and Esco watched as the other women formed like Voltron around Starr. Freeze's eyes grew cold as Sparkle and Glitter peeled the helmets off. Although they looked his way, one would not think they had ever met before, let alone had both their mouths on his cock at the same time. He was sure they had been given specific instructions to carry that way. He eyed them as they floated through the strip. His eyes were pulled in a different direction from the sound of his right-hand man's voice.

"That's her right?" Esco asked for a second time thinking Freeze had heard him.

"Her? Who?" He looked in the direction Esco was facing.

"Prime's bitch, from that night we were gonna pop on them clowns," Esco recapped the incident in a whisper.

Freeze ignored him. Instead, he locked eyes on Monica. The two also made brief eye contact. Seeing her with the Double Gs confirmed what he had thought that night. He was sure Prime had been the victim of the same heinous act he had endured. He studied her as Bubbles took her by one arm. Both women had a striking resemblance of beauty. The way they gracefully moved with hidden dominance was the same. All five of their backs turned to him and they strutted away into the trucks' high beams. They were immediately drowned by women in motorcycle jackets, sporting the most hated logo known to man.

These bitches gotta be stopped, was the only thought that flowed through Freeze's mind as he watched them spill into the gay club across the street like they owned not only the club, but the city of Las Vegas as well.

Over at Club Panties, Starr, Diamond, and Bubbles made their way down to the lower level of the establishment in the three-floor elevator.

"I promise you, you would have thought he seen a ghost." She continued her conversation about her and Freeze's brief exchange as they spilled out of the elevator. "You should have seen that nigga's face when he saw me." Starr chuckled as she was the first to sit.

Diamond and Bubbles both pulled out their respective chairs. They now all sat in a private section of Club Panties discussing and contemplating their next move while the rest of the members partied upstairs.

The words, *"We're supposed to be a ghost who haunts, not wolves who hunt,"* spoken by Queen Fem, invaded Starr's mind. Things had definitely begun to spiral out of control at a rapid pace, she thought. Nonetheless, she was confident it was not too late to repair the damage done already, especially since she had her own ace in the hole. Queen Fem was not the only one in the organization who had resources and connections in high places. Starr smiled at the thought of being able to handle the situation without running to Queen Fem. Although she loved Queen Fem like a mother, lately she had grown tired of seeking help and guidance from her like a little girl. *I'm a big girl,* she told herself as she changed subjects.

"On a positive note," Starr started out saying, "my insider informed me that this McCarthy guy has been removed from our case. The FBI's running scared. Thanks to you, of course, Diamond," she commended her, rubbing Diamond's thigh under the tablecloth.

"I wish I could've seen his face," Bubbles declared.

"He won't take this lying down, I'm sure, which leads me to my next topic of discussion." Starr leaned in closer and spoke lower and in a more subtle tone. "I'm beginning to take these claims of an agent among us to be the truth."

"Who do you think it could be?" Bubbles asked.

"I have my suspicions," Starr retorted. "After a few more tests, I'll have my answer. But, for now, watch what you say or do around anyone. And when the perpetrator is caught, I'll deal with her myself. I'll give her a fair chance to fight for her life, right before she begs me to end it," Starr proclaimed.

The other three women in the room nodded in agreement. They too wanted to know who the culprit was.

"Have you received any more calls?" Diamond asked.

"No." Starr shook her head. "And that's the crazy thing about this."

"Well, maybe it's a good thing. Maybe it was bogus," Bubbles joined in.

"No, it wasn't bogus. Too many things have been happening lately. Luckily we stay on top of our shit." Starr flashed a smirk. "With that being said, let's join the rest of our sisters and celebrate our minor victory," Starr chimed. "And where the hell is Felicia?" Starr questioned.

Bubbles shrugged as she stood, knowing the question was mainly directed to her. It was no secret that she and Felicia hung out the most out of all the other members.

"I was wondering the same thing," Diamond joined in as she backed away from the table. "Not like her to be late for a meeting."

"I was wondering why my fucking ears were ringing." Like magic, Felicia appeared out of nowhere with a partial smile plastered across her face.

"Where were you?" Starr looked down at her rose gold–toned Michael Kors.

"Putting everything together for that move you asked me to make," she reminded Starr.

Starr nodded, remembering. The answer went over both Diamond's and Bubbles's heads. Bubbles brushed it off but Diamond felt different. "Keeping secrets now, are we?" Her eyes shifted from Felicia to Starr.

"It was on a need-to-know basis," was all Starr offered, stone-faced. Her mood had instantly changed. She didn't appreciate Diamond's accusation and she wanted her to know.

"Oh, I guess I didn't need to know then." Diamond rolled her eyes, although she knew she was out of line. As soon as the words spilled out of her mouth she knew she was in error. "I didn't mean to say . . ." she attempted to clean up her response to Starr's answer.

She had let her emotions get the best of her and that was out of character for her. She was one who had mastered keeping a poker face at all times. But it was apparent that she had not quite mastered the art when it came to how she felt about Starr. Ever since the morning Starr had received the phone call while at her house, Diamond believed she was moving and acting differently. Even the last time they had been together, Diamond felt her lover was being distant despite the fact that she lay right next to her. There was no doubt in her mind that something was wrong but, whatever the case, still it didn't excuse the fact that Starr was her boss and what she said and how she chose to deal with something was what it was.

Both Felicia and Bubbles stood frozen and wide-eyed. Neither of the two knew how it had gone from zero to a hundred in a matter of seconds. They waited to see what Starr had to say.

The tension was thick enough to slice with a knife, as Starr sat there staring at Diamond as if she were a total stranger. It was as though everyone in the room was holding their breath until Starr spoke.

The longer Starr remained silent, the more Diamond had realized just how much she had crossed the line. "You gonna accept my apology?" She was conscious of the way in which she had asked. She knew how Starr was when it came to what and how a person talked to her. Her silence made Diamond feel uneasy. "Starrsh—"

"Apology accepted," Starr chimed in. She cut Diamond off before she could call out her full name. Her tone was subtle but bland, but she no longer felt the way she just had moments ago. It had been a long and stressful day as well as week for her and prior to her lover getting up under her skin, she was all too ready to have a good time. She stood up and pushed her chair away from the oval table.

"Now let's go enjoy ourselves," she advised with the same tone she had accepted Diamond's apology with as she led the way to the secret elevator. Diamond, Felicia, and Bubbles followed.

Each one of them was all too ready to head downstairs and get their party on.

Diamond caught up to Starr just as they reached the elevator. She came up alongside of her. "I really am sorry," Diamond whispered into her ear as she kissed Starr's outer lobe.

Starr turned her head in her direction. "I believe you." She smiled and nodded as the number one on the elevator lit up and the sliding door opened. Then she stepped inside and waited for her crew to follow suit.

Chapter Thirty

Officer Blake had strolled into work whistling tunes from his favorite song. The day had started out normal as any other had, except for him parking next to Officer Douglass's car. Blake always showed up before him because he didn't have a family. His job was his life. He liked to stay on top of things and get firsthand knowledge before roll call. He thought nothing of it. He got out of his Pontiac Gran Turismo and retrieved his bags from his truck, walked past Douglass's Dodge Magnum, and walked up the steps of the parking lot back entrance. He took a second to embrace that feeling he loved to live for. It was usually so quiet outside of the Thirty-fourth Street precinct station.

But all you got inside was organized madness. Phones were ringing, jokes were being cracked, complaints were being made by the weirdest-looking people, food was being passed, criminals were being cuffed and transported from room to room and cell to cell. The bullpens were packed. The Feds were there. *The Feds? Are here? Why?* he wondered.

Officer Blake looked toward the back. The door of Chief Andrews's office was wide open. One of the agents just happened to turn and catch eye contact with Blake. He looked down at the photo clipped to the right side of the folder and then back at Blake. He whispered something to the other agents in the room. By the way they all turned and looked in his direction, Blake didn't have to be a genius to know that the agent had said something about him. Officer Blake paused in his tracks. He had a bad feeling. Something told him he should turn around and hightail it up out the precinct. *Why run and look guilty? They could be here for anything,* he reasoned with himself.

He happened to look down the hall and spot two agents escorting his longtime partner out of the interrogation room in handcuffs. Officer Douglass had his head down but somehow their eyes happen to meet. Officer Blake saw the guilt written all over his partner's face. *What the fuck did you do?* Officer Douglass just dropped his head back to the ground as the agents guided him by the armpits. *Fucking piece of shit Judas.* There was no doubt in his mind that his partner had sold him out.

Officer Blake shook his head in disgust then slowly backed up. He looked straight and then from side to side. *It's now or never.* Blake dropped his bag and ran back toward the entrance of the precinct. He could hear his name being shouted in the distance behind him as he fled. As he reached the door, his hands trembled so much that he was unable to get his key into the lock. The whole set dropped to the concrete. Blake panicked. "Fuck," he cursed as he quickly kneeled to retrieve his keys from the ground. Luckily, he was successful at his second try. Just as he reached for the car door handle, two black GMC Suburbans skidded to a complete stop, blocking his car.

One of the SUVs managed to barricade Officer Blake between it and his vehicle as the other agents spilled out of the precinct backing up all bystanders. He didn't know what to do. A mixture of fear and anger overcame him. *I'm not going to fucking prison.* Blake did a quick scan of his surroundings. He knew he only had two options. He had already made his mind up that one of them was not an option at all. With that in mind, he drew his Glock .40 from his holster and opened fire into the SUV that had him pinned in. The agent driving the Suburban wasted no time putting the SUV in reverse.

The agents coming from the precinct ducked for cover. That was just enough time for Blake to take flight. He ran deep into the parking lot and began hiding behind cars. The other agents jumped out of the Suburbans with AR15s in hand and stood behind open doors. They swayed the fully automatic machine guns back and forth.

Officer Douglass couldn't believe the disaster. He was being pinned down to the ground with an agent over him, protecting him from getting shot. *Damn feds are robots.*

Blake was ducking behind the trunk of a Toyota Camry. He was breathing heavily as he opened the rotating barrel of his weapon. He confirmed that he only had five remaining shots left in his clip and the rest of his ammunition was in the bag he had dropped. There was no escaping. The parking lot was fenced in. He was surrounded by agents also ducking behind cars using hand signals to move in closer on him. There was nothing left to do but pray. He did a Hail Mary across his chest, kissed his curled index finger, pointed up at the sky, and then popped up, pointing his pistol at the first and closest agent. They both locked eyes and fingered their trigger simultaneously.

A single bullet sailed straight into the left side of Agent Kelly's forehead, knocking her off her feet as her gunfire sprayed high up into the air. Two of her wild shots managed to lodge themselves into Officer Blake. One tore into the right side of his neck while another ripped into his cheek. The impact slammed him back on the Nissan Maxima behind him. He was somehow still alive and held on to his firearm tightly. "Son of a bitch!" he cried out. He could feel the blood leaking from both his face and neck. *This is not how it supposed to end,* he decided. *I'm not going to be somebody's bitch in prison.* With that being his final thought, Officer Blake raised his weapon, stuck the barrel in his mouth, and blew his own brains out the back of his head.

Agents rushed over to both bodies. Agent Snyder kicked the pistol away from Officer Blake's bloody corpse. Another agent retrieved it and put it in a bag. They both strolled over to agent Kelly's lifeless body.

Douglass heard the panicking news of both deaths come over the agent who was guarding his radio. The agent who had him in custody shot him a look of disgust before he launched his attack. It came out of nowhere. Douglass was out cold before he even realized what had hit him. The smelling salts placed under his nose revived him. He woke up with his wrists cuffed to the Suburban's inside ceiling.

It took minutes for the words he was hearing to register. It would take hours for them to be verified as the truth. Agent McCarthy hadn't ever heard Chief Andrews's voice be anything other than smooth, calm, and under control. But what he just heard from him was tears as he tried to explain what happened without even knowing what went wrong. He heard the regret Chief Andrews felt in his tone through the phone. He listened as the chief beat himself up for not handling his problem in house, until it worked its way up to federal status.

The news about them taking McCarthy off the case was also an issue for him. It didn't sit too well. He had been personally dealing with Agent McCarthy for several years. The two knew where each other stood at all times. Had he known Agent McCarthy would be removed from the case he would have never handed over Officers Douglass and Blake; he was sure of that. He was now feeling that the whole investigation could blow back in his face. But it was too late. Just as he finished making a personal copy of the taped confession, he saw a group of men dressed in black suits and ties headed in the direction of his office. "I gotta call you back," Chief Andrews informed McCarthy before abruptly hanging up.

Agent McCarthy hung up knowing their rela-

tionship could never be the same. He was so furious at Mobley for pulling him off the case. He felt there was no way he would have allowed such a massacre to happen. His approval would've been much different, more subtle. He knew exactly what Reddick had done. Trying to solidify himself as the new agent in charge, he stormed into the precinct spreading orders around without any plan or strategy.

McCarthy flopped back down into his chair and buried his face into his hands with his elbows pointed high up into the air. His own eyes began to water as he thought of Agent Jody Kelly. She was with the Bureau for a little over six years. She was tough, always trying to prove that she could hang with the rest of the big boys. Agent McCarthy shook his head at yet another fallen agent on his side of the team. It was evident the Double Gs were not playing fair and had no remorse or regard for his colleagues' lives. He knew he had to do something before many more lost their lives.

Agent Mobley was in his eleventh-floor office when he got the news of the unfortunate tragedy. Instant anger set in, but he had to stick with his decision. Agent Reddick wasn't to blame. But one thing for sure, somebody had to pay, and it had to start with the root of it all. There was only one fall guy remaining in the picture and they had him in custody.

How did this go so wrong? Douglass cried to himself in disbelief. He realized he had just committed suicide in a much different way from his partner. He had caused all of this for nothing, he told himself for the umpteenth time as the chain of events unraveled right before his very eyes. He was left to take the weight for it all; everything he had confessed to was now stuck to him. He was no longer the snitch. Instead of immunity, he was sure he would get the death penalty and spend his time waiting for execution boxed in an underground cell in an ADX maximum federal prison facility and his outside contact would be restricted.

He looked around the frigid room. There was nothing. No windows; just four walls, a concrete bed, and no sheets or blanket. To top it off, the cell was freezing cold and, because he was on suicide watch, he was dressed in only a paper suit. He hadn't even been transported from the federal building yet. No one said a word to him. Although he had been spit on, called every derogatory word known to mankind, and badly beaten while he was in the bullpen, he knew the worst was yet to come.

Chapter Thirty-one

The following Friday evening, Bubbles was in the back of the stretch Escalade sitting next to Starr. They were being chauffeured to Club Panties, while Starr discussed the latest chain of events with Diamond, who was stuck at the office. By special request of Starr, Felicia was in the second Escalade riding with Monica and the twins, who were all surprised to be invited to make the grand entrance. And as usual they were surrounded by the Double G bikes.

"You knew somehow this was all going to fall back on us. Things are getting too hectic," Starr spoke into the phone receiving the news of what had happened to Agent Kelly. "Three agents are dead in the same week."

"But that had nothing to do with us," Diamond rationalized.

"In the end, it does. If Douglass was going to roll over on Blake, he had to throw in information on us to sweeten the deal!"

"Yeah, but all he could admit is what they did. As usual nothing physically traces back to us. That's how it's always been. So they had nothing. Maybe things will lighten up with that McCarthy guy off the case."

"Guys like him don't just lie down. He's a tough agent, Diamond. He's even more dangerous to us now because he doesn't have a leash. It's time to clean up. Tomorrow we start clipping all loose ends. All of them." The tone in her command was unmistakable.

"What do you suggest?"

"I'll fill you in tomorrow. I'm putting in the call tonight. It's time for a few members to pay some dues. I'm using one of them for a specific task. It's time to start weeding out the garden. I have another message that needs to be sent. This Douglass guy caused us some real unnecessary problems. Officer Blake was a good asset. Douglass needs to pay."

"I'm sure you'll come up with something nice for him," Diamond whispered in a devilish tone.

"Actually, even worse. I'm leaving it up to Queen."

"Uh-oh, he's in trouble."

"Not just him, my dear, not just him."

"I have to go. US Attorney Linda McCarthy is back."

Both women disconnected the call. Starr turned her attention back to Bubbles. "Soon as we get into the club, escort Monica to my office. And I don't want to be disturbed."

Bubbles nodded. She was not clear on the mission, but she believed there was one. *Why else would she want Monica?* Bubbles thought as her instructions were given to her. As far as she was concerned it involved somebody getting their hands dirty.

Chapter Thirty-two

It had been a very long day for Agent McCarthy. He walked into his home feeling defeated. As soon as he cleared the door and was in the foyer, he removed his blazer, untied his tie, and unbuttoned his shirt, walking across the polished wooden floor until he entered the living room and into the kitchen where he could see his lovely wife Linda, circling the kitchen. She hadn't heard him come in. He slowly crept up on her.

"Hey, honey," she called out when she felt his presence before he could reach her.

He walked up on her and pecked her on the cheek. "Where's Charley?" he asked, referring to their nine-year-old daughter, Charlene.

"She's upstairs washing up for dinner. I told the sitter I'd feed her. She wasn't feeling too well. Ugh, I'm back," she continued. "I just got in not even fifteen minutes ago. I had a long day at the office. There's a major trial coming up. You know that Spalding guy, the one who knocked off like ten banks? Okay, yeah, them," she answered before he could confirm his recollection. "So anyway, as if unbelievably making bail wasn't good enough for them, they're actually taking this to trial. My guess is it's an attempt to make the government spend hard-earned taxpayers' money, or confiscated drug money," she continued, which was completely ignored as she rambled while multitasking with the dishes and prepping for dinner. "We'll have them dead tonight. The only thing that scares me is their lawyer. This Morgan. Diamond Morgan. She's undefeated and so was I until I met her. She gets me every time."

The name Diamond Morgan stood out to him. He was trying to place where he had heard it from. "Diamond Morgan?" McCarthy let the name dance around in his head. Then it dawned on him. "That's the hotshot attorney who came prancing her way through the office," he remembered. "And she mentioned you, too. The way she mentioned you all makes sense now." He drew a conclusion.

"What all makes sense?" A confused look appeared on Linda McCarthy's face.

"How you two would know each other and the fact that she knew I was your husband," he replied.

"Yes, we're very familiar with each other."
Linda McCarthy scowled. "You know her too,"
she added. "Or at least you should, anyway," she
believed.

"How so?" Now it was McCarthy who had a
confused look on his face.

"I talk about her all the time, but you never
listen, do you? No, you just let me ramble while
you rub my hair and then, you know, we switch
subjects," she stated with a flirtatious smirk,
looking sexy as ever.

"I've been meaning to ask you about her. She's
the one that got Pearson out of my custody.
Is she really that good?" He both wanted and
needed to know. He was hopeful that the rumor
was a joke. If anybody knew about the attorney, it would be his wife. Like himself, Linda
McCarthy made it her business to stay abreast
on any- and everything in her profession. If
Diamond Morgan was as good as he had recently
heard, there was no way his wife would not be
familiar with her competitor. After all, she too
was known as a shark in the courtrooms.

"Honey, I'm on the government's side. I'm the
top attorney for the prosecutor's office. Hell, it's
like we make the rules. At least dictate 'em. But
she beats me every time we go up against each
other, one of a kind. She's definitely the best

I've seen in a long time. Don't get me wrong, she knows her stuff, but everything else happens in her favor. Between witnesses not appearing in court and missing evidence, some of the cases we've beat ourselves." Linda McCarthy shook her head submissively.

"Linda, I believe she's one of them."

"One of them? Like who is them?"

"One of the goddamn Double Gs," McCarthy boomed.

"The gay bike group you've been obsessing over and telling me about?" his wife questioned. A puzzled look took over her face. She was curious to know how her husband had drawn such a conclusion.

"Yeah, the dykes!" he exclaimed.

"Honey, don't be silly. And please don't talk like that. It makes you sound like you're homophobic," Linda McCarthy defended. "You remember the last time the guy tried to file prejudice and defamation of character charges against you for that statement you made that was taken out of context?" she reminded him.

"Really, Linda? Homophobic?" Agent McCarthy was agitated. "And you know that complaint was bullshit." He couldn't believe she had gone there. "Okay, excuse the fuck out of me, but explain me this," McCarthy began to ramble. "How the hell did she find out and get to us so quick? And, she was determined to keep Pearson's mouth shut," he pointed out.

"Tom, relax," she dismissed his words. "But if you really would like to know, that's what lawyers do. It's what they get paid for." She poked a hole in her husband's theory.

McCarthy shook his head. "That's the thing," he began. "Pearson doesn't have anywhere near that kind of money for such a high-profile lawyer like you just described." He continued to shake his head in disbelief. "It just doesn't add up. I've been through her financial records and everything, Lin." He thought about it. "You ever see or hear of this Morgan gal having any affiliation with a gang? Hell, do you know whether she has a boyfriend?" He wanted to know whatever his wife knew about the woman who put a damper on his investigation and had gotten him removed from it.

Linda thought for a second. "Nothing much, other than the usual and normal comparisons to me as being someone to be reckoned with in those courtrooms." She told him all of what she knew about Diamond Morgan. "She's pretty private. Most of 'em are. I'm the only one with a hotshot agent. They think I get all the action," she joked.

Any other time, he would've laughed at his wife's dry humor, but he stayed serious. "Yeah, well, she's been linked to that club of theirs and she's not even hiding it."

"Wow! Well hopefully y'all take 'em down soon, so I can start being the most feared prosecutor again. Right now, it's her time."

"I'm working on it," he declared. He was tempted to let her know that he was thrown off the case due to Diamond's work but didn't feel like getting into it.

"When's the funeral?" Linda asked. She seasoned the fish fillet strips she was about to bake.

"Oh! That reminds me. I need you to go with me tomorrow. The Bureau is paying for all three of the burials, so they kind of rushed Agent Kelly's burial process. She didn't need one. The family agreed. It saved everyone money. The Bureau has so much money and they don't spend a damn dime that they don't have to, not even for their own. They're dead, for Christ's sake!"

"Honey, you're talking about the same branch of government that formed the CIA."

"Yeah, and with the same corruption," Agent McCarthy stated under his breath.

The thought made him wonder. There were things during his investigation that McCarthy just couldn't explain. It was the first time he had actually noticed that the closer he got to gaining more information on the Double Gs the more the evidence continued to slip right between his fingers. It seemed as if they stayed one to three steps ahead of him. Despite being snatched off the case and claiming to not care anymore, McCarthy had a strong urge to find out just how connected his targets really were.

Chapter Thirty-three

Starr and the rest of the Double Gs sat in the luxurious comfort of the upper deck VIP lounge, sipping drinks and making light conversation as four exotic female strippers danced and performed sexual acts in front of them. The dancers fondled and kissed each other while some of the Double G members showered them with money. Some of the others groped their breasts and asses while they shoved bills into the dancers' tops and G-strings. Starr sat between Felicia and Monica. Her hand was rested on Monica's left thigh the entire time. The three of them were clearly tipsy and Starr was turned on, ready to play. Without Diamond around, she was lonely. Although she and Diamond weren't exclusive or restricted to each other, they were still very much in love.

Tonight was about testing. Starr leaned in to whisper into Monica's ear. "Monica, meet me in my office and wait for me. I need to speak to you about something. I'll be right behind you," she proclaimed.

Without hesitation, Monica stood up, pulled the fallen straps of her silver silk Chanel thin dress back up over her shoulders and then provocatively strutted her way down the hall. She could feel that the three glasses of Cîroc on the rocks she'd had had started to take effect by the way she slightly staggered down the hall.

Starr turned to Felicia. "Listen. I'm putting you on her tomorrow okay?"

Felicia thought of asking why, but she knew better than to question Starr. So she just listened as she continued.

"I'm sending you two on an important mission. I can't use any of the guys from the files for this. This has to come directly from us. Now, you're just tagging along. Make sure she's the one who puts in the real work. The first thing I want you to do is take her out to our firing range in the morning, see what she's made of, so we'll know if we have to go another route. Report her accuracy to me and then your assignment will come through the phone. I'm counting on you, Felicia; don't let her fuck this one up. I need her to stay as close to me as possible until I find out exactly what's what. But my guess is either way it goes we probably gonna have to get rid of her."

She seductively rubbed on Felicia's left leg. "Now, too much business is boring. I'm 'bout to go have some real fun." Starr gave Felicia a passionate kiss before she stood. They smiled at each other. It was no secret. Before there was Diamond, it was Felicia, so none of the Double Gs were surprised by the exchange. Besides, even if they wanted to say anything, they knew better not to. Not that Starr was concerned. She had long ago established a "see no evil, hear no evil, speak no evil" policy in the organization. She gazed into Felicia's eyes for a moment. There was a brief pause. A new thought had entered her mind. She smiled at the thought. "Care to join me?" She reached out her hand for Felicia.

Felicia took hold of it and shook her head. "Here we go again." Felicia chuckled.

Starr guided her up and then escorted her to her office where Monica awaited.

On the opposite side, the action going on across the street was a little different. As usual, Freeze was mentally distant, but his crew was used to it. Most of them remembered being the same way throughout all of their years in the DFY prison. They understood that a lot of his anger and aggression was pinned up inside him. But they didn't know the half. There were secrets, so many of them. Deep, dark ones that; sometimes, the mind played tricks. There was one thing about Freeze's mind that wasn't screwed up: his memory. He never forgot a face. Even if that wasn't the case, he would always remember Officer Blake's or Officer Douglass's. It was Officer Blake who he had shot at when he was at Frenchie's house. It was Officer Douglass who carried him away and charged him with the crimes that sent him away, depriving him of his final stage of his childhood, turning him into the monster of a killer he had become today. Seeing what had happened to them on the news was exciting to him and depriving. The story of what happened to Officer Blake was very entertaining to Freeze. On the other hand, he despised Officer Douglass and the way he dragged him out of that house with no remorse, for being the cause of the split among his only remaining family members.

"Your table's ready," one of the promoters informed Freeze as he and his entourage reached the front entrance of the hot spot.

"Good looking." Freeze shook the man's hand, pressing four crisp hundred dollar bills in his palm on behalf of himself and all twelve of his goons.

The promoter nodded and smiled. "Anytime, Freeze." He didn't bother to look at the money. Instead he slipped it into his inside suit jacket pocket.

The sound of Rick Ross's voice filled the air, catching Freeze's attention. One would have thought the party was outside, the way the track "Ima Boss" rang out. When he looked he noticed where the music was coming from.

Prime had made quite an entrance himself. His team pulled up back to back in a long line of exotic vehicles. They rolled like superstars. Freeze had never seen the convoy of cars and SUVs pull up. People cheered them on as doors flew open in front of valet. Prime was the first to exit his calypso red Jaguar. The rest of his crew followed suit. He waited until they had all possied up around him. They hovered around Prime like he was Barack Obama himself; then, together, they walked past the long line of people who hadn't made it in Treasures yet due to the maximum capacity set by the fire marshal or their suburban status.

They were shouted out by the DJ as they entered. "Make way for the boss man and his crew, y'all. We got some serious money in the house tonight, ladies and gents. Don't go broke tryin'a keep up. Let's just say that they leave for us ta sweep up!" DJ Odyssey clowned into the mic as all eyes watched Prime and his crew roll upstairs to the VIP lounge.

As they were escorted to their personal section, Prime briefly locked eyes with Freeze; when they both let it go, they figured that their day to clash would eventually come. But for now they both felt that they had more important things to concentrate on. They had no way of knowing their thoughts actually intertwined. Freeze couldn't help but chuckle to himself. He assumed that Prime had endured the same humiliation and degrading experience he had. *If only muthafuckas knew,* thought Freeze. He waved down one of the half-naked waitresses then sent her over to Prime's section to inform him that he was picking up their tab for the night.

Prime felt that he couldn't let Freeze show him up like that. So he told the waitress to inform them that he would be doing the same for them. It was a statement that quickly turned into a drinking contest. Both crews got turned up with no limitation. Most of the bottles were either passed out to strangers or poured on the strippers. Both men eyed the other for the rest of the evening as their crew lived it up at their expense. By the end of the night, Freeze and Prime gave each other approving nods. Freeze made a mental note to do a follow-up on the acknowledging nod. For some reason, he had a funny feeling that another time and another place he and Prime should have a sit-down and talk. Unbeknownst to him, Prime was thinking the same thing.

Chapter Thirty-four

At first Monica felt she was stuck between a rock and a hard place. When she was summoned by Starr, she immediately became nervous. The look on Bubbles's face when she had told her only added to her nervousness. For the life of her she couldn't think of anything she had done to jeopardize her position in the organization. As far as she was concerned, she had proven herself and was now a Double G. The walk to Starr's office seemed to end too quick. She abruptly stopped in front of the huge wooden stained door. She still hadn't come up with a valid reason why Starr would want to see her in her office. She knocked on it rapidly in succession. She heard the voice on the other side of it telling her to come in. When she did, to her surprise, Felicia sat off to the right of Starr.

"Enjoying yourself?" Starr asked.

"Yes, thank you." Monica nodded.

"Good. Good to hear." Starr looked her up and down as she spoke.

Monica could feel her eyes undressing her. Instantly the nature of her visit to the office became clear. She glanced over at Felicia, who also was giving her body a full survey.

Are you fucking serious? Monica couldn't believe the predicament she was in. The scenery had her feeling uneasy. She felt like a piece of meat and Starr and Felicia intended to be the bread.

"You okay?" Starr asked. She titled her head to the side.

Monica knew she was analyzing her. "Um hm." She nodded for a second time.

Their eyes met. She could see the lustful flames burning inside of Starr's eyes as she stared into them. She had no clue how she was going to get herself out of it. But she was willing to do whatever it took. Solving the death of her brother meant more to her than anything else in the world, even her own life.

"Come here." It was more of a command rather than a request.

Monica embraced the gesture with reluctance, more so because of Felicia's presence, but within minutes she let her guard down and charted new territory. Although she considered herself to be a heterosexual female, she was no stranger to a woman's touch. It had been a long time since she experienced that feeling. She was much younger the last time it had happened. Since then, she had become only curious, never acting on it. Monica's thoughts flashed back to when she was a young, promiscuous teen, living in that big, old, unfamiliar house where she first met Sara.

They were the same age. They used to do everything together: eat, sleep in the same room, make up and dress their dolls for hours. They spent more time together than apart. As their bodies changed and began to develop so did their hormones. They were fifteen the first time they had explored any sexual interests toward the other. They started hiding in the closet kissing and caressing, fondling and fingering. What started out as an experiment quickly grew into a passion, a craving, a preference. Ultimately, their brief childhood love affair came to an end after Sara's mother caught them in the act. After that, they had never seen or heard from one another again, but the sweet memories were never erased from Monica's mind.

Now, those feelings had been awakened. The fire between her legs had ignited and resurfaced the moment Starr's lips made contact with hers. The smooth sound of Jill Scott filled the air as Starr's tongue probed Monica's mouth. While she enjoyed the kiss, she couldn't help but notice Felicia slide to the left of Starr and begin to suck on her neck. Felicia stared at her as she planted gentle kisses and licked Starr's collar. It turned Monica on. She watched with lustful eyes as Felicia's hands made their way up to her breasts. Felicia caressed Monica's breasts through the silk fabric of her dress. Her perky nipples poked through the thin garment. Monica closed her eyes as the back of Felicia's busy right hand glided against her breast also. Starr continued to kiss her passionately the whole while. She could feel Starr's hand massaging her sex through the fabric. Her touch enhanced Monica's moistness.

She hadn't been this turned on in a long time. Monica's kiss became aggressive. The familiar feeling had taken charge and control over her. What she had once buried deeply she now longed for. She caught Starr by surprised when she broke their lip lock and grabbed for her dress. Starr smiled as Monica took both of her hands and hiked the bottom of Starr's dress up to her thin waistline. Monica slowly slithered down between Starr's knees. She stared up at Starr with lustful eyes. Starr flashed a half of a smile as Monica licked her lips seductively. Monica then broke her stare and lowered her gaze as she dropped her head between Starr's legs. Felicia watched as Monica slid Starr's panties down her legs and ankles. The sweet smell of Bath & Body Works filled the air. Monica spread Starr's muscular, thick thighs even farther apart. She used her fingers to gently part the outer lips of Starr's clean-shaven, glistening cave. Just as Monica began to indulge in the urge to taste her, Felicia dropped to her knees, right next to her. Starr cooed and cleared her desk in one sweep. She hiked herself onto it and spread her legs wider.

Monica and Felicia exchanged an intimate kiss in front of Starr's exposed clit. Starr could feel the heat between her legs from Felicia's and Monica's breath. Monica ended the kiss between her and Felicia. She then turned and buried her face between Starr's inner thighs. She licked and sucked Starr's honey-flavored pussy, sending her into a chilling whirlwind of ecstasy. Monica was enjoying pleasuring Starr so much that she never noticed Felicia sliding behind her. She moaned from the two fingers Felicia inserted into her wetness. Felicia wasted no time removing Monica's panties. Within minutes, they were all engrossed in a ménage à trois.

"Yeah, suck that shit!" Starr demanded. She pushed Monica's face deeper into her pussy. Monica began to angrily suck on Starr's wet-

ness like she had never done before. Felicia
had caused herself to orgasm from sucking on
Monica. It was like a drug. She kept slurping
and drinking the orgasms she brought Monica
to as Monica ground back and forth on her face.
Starr couldn't take it anymore. Strangely, she
now wanted Monica all to herself. She broke up
the party for a slight second. She pushed Monica
from between her legs and sat on the side of the
desk. Felicia removed her head from between
Monica's legs.

"Thank you. That will be all." She calmly
directed her words to Felicia with a smile.

Felicia wiped her mouth, stood up, looked at
the both of them while fixing her clothes, and
then returned the smile. She strutted toward the
door. The loud roar of the music spilled in for a
second as she opened and shut the door behind
her.

Starr turned to Monica with the most seduc-
ing gaze in her eyes, ready to take back full control. She approached Monica until she was mere
inches away from her.

"Now, where were we?"

Chapter Thirty-five

I couldn't have returned at a better time,
Felicia thought as she reemerged into the main
part of the club. DJ Franzen, who was one of the
hottest DJs in Las Vegas, was going in on
the turntables. One of J. Cole's popular tracks
was blended and mixed in with one of Kendrick
Lamar's. Felicia smiled and shook her head as
she peered over at her crew's VIP section. The
Double Gs were turned all the way up and she
knew exactly why. Over two dozen plus-sized
women tossed back bottles of assorted flavors
of Cîroc, rosé, Patrón, and Ace of Spades while
they tossed money in the air and chanted their
favorite song in unison. Every dancer in the club
was in the vicinity of the Double Gs. Women
twerked, booty bounced, popped, and exercised
their acrobatic skills while the Double Gs turned
Club Panties into a night straight out of the play-
book of the infamous ATL strip club Magic City.

Felicia danced her way over to join her crew. The spotlight found its way on her as she bounced through the club. She could hear the familiar beat coming to her and the rest of the Double Gs' favorite turn-up song as she snapped both her fingers and hips to the blend of the current and upcoming tracks DJ Franzen spun.

"Shout out to my homegirls Starr, Felicia, Bubbles, and the rest of the Double Gs," DJ Franzen announced. "I know this y'all shit right here!" The DJ spun the song back and started it from the beginning.

Felicia threw an acknowledging hand in the air, while the other Double Gs went crazy hearing the shout out. She noticed Bubbles had done the same from where she stood, moving her back in a snake motion in VIP.

The bouncer dressed in all black removed the velvet rope for Felicia. She gave a courtesy nod as she walked past him. She was handed a bottle of Peach Cîroc by Sparkle and smothered with a bear hug from Glitter, as they all continued to chant the chorus of their anthem. It was evident to Felicia that the twins and everybody else was bloody from the alcohol, not to mention the strong smell of some of Cali's finest bud in the immediate area. Felicia took a long swig of the bottle before joining her girls.

"'Watch out for the big girls! Watch out for the big girls!'" The hook of the popular house music song repeated over and over as the Double Gs stomped their feet to the beat. They became even more hyped as the chorus switched. Some of the Double Gs had grabbed hold of some of the dancers and started pumping them from the back to the beat of the song while other Double Gs cheered them on.

"'Big girls, big, big girls, big girls, big, big girls,'" filled the air as the Double Gs dominated the club.

The thunderous music had all of the Double G members lit. Everyone was in a zone as they tossed back shots of Patrón and nursed liters of assorted flavors of Sean Puffy Combs's popular vodka. Had they not been so turned up, they may have been more on point.

"Team Alpha, are you in position?" the lead SWAT Agent asked from the van.

"Roger that," the reply came through the radio.

"Team Charlie, are you in position?" he asked.

"Set to engage," the agent confirmed.

"On my mark," the lead agent ordered.

The numbers one through three were counted down before the lead SWAT agent gave the green light to move in.

As the song came to an end so did the Double Gs. Felicia sat beside Bubbles while some of members slid off to the back with dancers for lap dances, while others paired up and doubled teamed some of the other ones.

"Did you enjoy yourself back there?" Bubbles asked somewhat enviously. She actually liked Monica and wished she had been the one offered the opportunity to visit Starr's office.

Felicia chuckled. "What are you talkin' about?"

"Fee, don't play. I smell pussy all over you."

Bubbles's comment caused Felicia to double over with laughter.

"At least tell me, was she any good?" Bubbles wanted to know.

"I can't really say. Starr kicked me out; wanted her all to herself." Felicia smiled.

Bubbles shook her head and snatched up her bottle of Red Berry Cîroc. "Being the boss has its perks," she said before taking a swig of the vodka.

"I'll drink to that," Felicia agreed.

The two friends tapped their bottles together and then tossed them back. The sudden loud noise startled them. The sound of shattered glassed could be heard as both of their Cîroc bottles hit the club floor simultaneously. The multiple red dots illuminating on their chests was enough to make them both hit the deck and take cover.

Within seconds a barrage of SWAT bombarded Club Panties. Flashlights were being shined, infrared beams crisscrossed, and assault weapons were being waved around as they filled the club. The music abruptly stopped and all that could be heard was the commotion of screams, broken bottles, and feet scurrying throughout the establishment. The scenery resembled a stampede or a bull run, thought Agent Reddick.

"Round up as many Double Gs as possible," he ordered. He smiled at the pun. He then made his way to the back where he figured he could find who he was looking for.

Meanwhile, downstairs, Starr massaged Monica's natural silky hair as the leader of the Double Gs brought her to yet another orgasm. Between the melodic sounds of Raheem DeVaughn and the pleasure Starr was creating, Monica felt as if she was in heaven. She knew she was in violation for many different reasons, but had no intention of stopping. She had let both her hair and her guard down and let go. *Her tongue is magical,* she thought, getting caught up in the matrix of what Starr was doing to her. She tossed her head back with closed eyes and bit down on her bottom lip.

Starr toyed with Monica's nipples while she expertly performed oral on her. She could feel her phone vibrating up against her hip, but she paid it no mind. She was in a zone and refused to let anything or anyone take her out of it. Had she decided to retrieve the phone and look at her screen, it may have made a difference. The two of them were so in tune with one another that they hadn't realized they weren't alone until the music stopped and was replaced with a voice.

"Sorry to break up your little soiree, ladies," Agent Reddick sarcastically remarked. He knew the clearing of his throat would get their attention.

Starr looked up at Monica and grimaced. She then calmly rose and slowly turned around. Monica sat up and covered her exposed body with her hands. The beams from the assault rifles swayed back and forth in their direction. Agent Reddick was smiling, holding up a warrant.

"I've been told I have bad timing," Agent Reddick joked. "But the problem is I have a piece of paper here that requires me to take care of this now. Well, with the time stamp and all. By the way, no need to call Ms. Morgan as of yet. This is strictly by the book." Agent Reddick flashed a smug look. "Get the one who was on top!" he yelled out to the first agent as the lights came on.

"Don't touch me!" Starr spat, pulling away from the agent.

He stood there dumbfounded, looking back and forth from Starr to his superior. Agent Reddick grimaced. He waved the agent off. Just then a female agent, Constanza, pushed her way through the madness and into the office.

"They're going crazy out there. There are all sorts of drugs on the floor." She drew her attention to Starr. "Since nobody's claiming anything and this is your establishment everything belongs to you."

Starr ignored the agent and continued to dress. Monica was more than embarrassed. But she was even more furious at the fact that she hadn't received the heads-up on the raid. She couldn't believe the humiliating position she was currently in.

"I'd like to see the warrant," Starr calmly requested.

"Sure, and Agent Constanza will read you your rights while you're doing so," Agent Reddick declared, pointing to the woman agent.

"Am I under arrest?" Starr asked.

"Just for now. I'm sure you'll be out soon, though. There's not enough here to stick, but we figured we'd start pushing back, letting you know who's boss." He turned his back on Starr and faced the SWAT team of agents.

Agent Constanza walked up to Starr. "This is for Agent Kelly!" She raised the back of her hand up at her. Her attempt was too slow and sloppy.

Starr weaved away from the intended blow. Raising the back of her own hand, she counteracted and delivered an alarming blow as her massive hand came crashing down on the side of Agent Constanza's face. The smack sent the agent flying to the ground. "Don't you ever raise your motherfuckin' hand up at me again in your life." Starr's words echoed through the office.

Two members of the SWAT team immediately rushed her and grabbed her from behind. To add insult to injury, Starr spat on the female agent while kicking wildly in the air as the two muscular agents subdued her. She was so out of control, she hadn't realized her cell phone slipped out of her pocket. And neither did any of the agents. They were all still trying to figure out how Agent Constanza wound up on the floor, holding the side of her face.

Monica noticed it. Her attention was still fixed on Starr and the ruckus she had caused. The office was instantly filled with a roomful of shocked faces.

Monica didn't know what to do. She just stood there in awe. She couldn't believe Starr's reaction.

Agent Reddick's back was turned so he hadn't seen what had just taken place. Everything had happened so quickly. He spun back around at the sound of Starrshma Fields's voice. He saw Agent Constanza on the ground and Starr being detained. Starr shot him a murderous look. "You better put a leash on that bitch," Starr growled as her blood continued to boil.

Agent Constanza slowly returned to her feet, rubbing her cheek from the sting. She wiped the dripping spit from the crevice of the right side of her mouth.

"Add that to your list of charges." Starr directed her sarcasm to the agent.

"You cunt-sucking bitch!" Now it was Agent Constanza who had to be detained by her peers.

Not a small or timid woman herself, it took every bit of her colleagues' strength to withhold her from the attack she nearly launched on

Starr. It took a minute for her to recover from the assault. The blow had dazed her, which had delayed her from springing right back up after Starr had knocked her down.

"Get off of me!" She twisted and turned as the two men struggled to contain her.

"Agent Constanza!" Reddick's voice boomed.

Her superior's voice caught her attention. Huffing and puffing, she snapped her neck in his direction.

"Calm yourself," he instructed.

Constanza rolled her eyes. She inhaled then let out the longest deep sigh she had ever taken in her life. "I'm fine."

The two agents began to release her slowly. She shrugged them off, then zeroed in on Starr. "This ain't over," she told her.

"Hope not." Starr gritted her teeth.

"Get her the hell out of here! Now!" Reddick yelled, as Starr giggled while being escorted past the agent she had just assaulted. Reddick walked over to Constanza. "You okay?"

"Aside from my ego being bruised. Sure, I'm cool." She flashed a reassuring smile.

"What about her?" one of the agents asked, pointing to Monica, who had just buttoned the last button of her blouse.

Agent Reddick stared over at Monica for a few seconds. She returned the eye contact. A look of disgust appeared across her face. She rolled her eyes at him right before turning her head away from him.

Shaking his head, he snickered. "Let her go. We got who we came for. Get her out of here and tear this place apart!" he then yelled.

Monica kneeled down and gathered up the rest of her belongings.

As Starr was escorted out of her office, she took in all of the chaos. The club had been turned upside down. Agents were everywhere, flipping up everything that wasn't nailed down. All of the club attendants had been harassed and kicked out into the street. She scanned the club infested with law enforcement. She didn't see Felicia or Bubbles anywhere, but could see some of the Double Gs all posted up, legs spread, facing the wall with palm flesh against it, while others were already handcuffed and being whisked out of the club. She was steaming on the inside at the scenery, but she refused to give the pigs who ran up in her establishment the satisfaction of seeing her react or respond. She knew they didn't have anything on any of her crew members, so that was the least of her concerns. Her mind was more focused on what they did or didn't have on her.

As she was escorted outside, the scene was even worse. Everyone from Treasures had come outside to see what was going on. They all stood in silence as Starr was brought out in her revealing clothes. She held her head high despite looking a mess. She smiled inside at the sight of Felicia and Bubbles. She managed to make eye contact with Felicia just before she reached the awaiting vehicle. Starr gave her a knowing head nod. Felicia caught it and tapped Bubbles. Starr watched as the two quickly disappeared into the crowd. Seconds later, she was being thrown in the back of a black Yukon Denali. She noticed a convoy of at least a dozen more SUVs. She was sure they were filled with Double Gs. She shook her head and smiled to herself at the new chain of events. "Let the games begin," Starr mumbled under her breath as she was whizzed away.

A Couple Hours Later

"I had to," Monica chimed into the phone as Agent McCarthy sat on the other end of the receiver in disbelief. She hated that she had to call and drop the bomb she just had about not only sleeping with Starr, but also getting caught by Agent Reddick and the other agents.

When she had calmed down, she realized why she hadn't been given the heads-up. Agent McCarthy's daughter was ill.

She had felt bad for forgetting. Just as she felt bad about reaching out to him now. She knew he wouldn't be pleased to hear what she had done to maintain her cover. "How's your daughter?" she asked.

"She's a strong girl, but I don't want to talk about that right now." He switched back to what she had just revealed to him. "What do you mean you had to? No, you didn't." His tone came across like a parent scolding a child.

"Yes, I did," she disagreed with him. "You told me to do whatever it took and I did. You knew it might come to that when you sent me on this mission. But, relax, it paid off. I have something nobody knows about. I'll bring it to you when the coast is clear. Let's just wait to see what happens now."

"Does she trust you?" he asked.

"Now more than ever," she said with confidence. "I have another mission tomorrow."

"Well, take advantage of the situation and get in deeper."

"Okay," she whispered. "I have to go. I'll fill you in later."

Chapter Thirty-six

The McCarthys arrived at the funeral a little late after dealing with the sickness of their daughter. He pulled up and parked behind a long line of cars. The three of them got out and walked down the lengthy cement path outside of the beautiful grass field until they met up with two or more people in black attire. There were reserved white plastic folding chairs for the McCarthys up front. The caskets were closed due to the damage the agents' bodies had received during their deaths. They were lined up side by side and covered with American flags. Huge pictures of them sat on top of the flags. Nearly two dozen soldiers stood in formation behind the caskets, with their wooden rifles against their chest, awaiting the twenty-one-gun salute ceremony in honor of the fallen agents. Head Agent Mobley stood at the podium. He turned and faced the mourning families and offered his deepest condolences. All three agents' families were filled with tears and were grief-stricken.

After Head Agent Mobley finished his speech he leaned into Agent McCarthy.

"That son of a bitch Douglass!" he cursed in McCarthy's ear. "All of his cases will be reversed. And, somehow, he still pulled off a deal for immunity. No justice, Tom. No justice. Sometimes I second-guess which side of the law I'm on."

"Me too," Agent McCarthy agreed.

Chapter Thirty-seven

The small cell was frigid. The central air had been purposely turned up to the maximum setting to provide extreme discomfort. She wasn't given a bedrail like the others who came through the intake process. The thin, hard plastic cot and the metal sink and toilet unit were the only three things in the cell besides her orange jumpsuit–covered body. She could hear the officers discussing her name outside the door right before a small slot was opened for her to stick her hands through to get cuffed.

"Fields, legal visit," the officer announced. Starr rolled her eyes as she stuck her wrists through the door's hole. The cold steel clamped down tightly, cutting off her blood circulation.

"Motherfucka," she mumbled.

The officer heard her and chuckled. "Come on, a tough gal like yourself? I'm sure you and your friends are used to playing with toys like these."

"Yeah, and ugly, fat, balding crackers are the reason why!" she retorted while exiting the cell.

She was led down the long hallway and steered into a small room with glass windows dividing it. Diamond pointed to the black phone, signaling her to pick it up. The door shut behind her for privacy. The cuffs stayed on for safety, and not hers. Both women cracked a forced, artificial smile before speaking.

"How're they treating you?" Diamond asked knowing the answer.

"Like shit. It's cool. I can handle it." Starr forced another smile. "What's the status?"

"Well, they're just being a bunch of hard asses. It's nothing serious. It's all theatre for the public eye. Making it look like they're at least trying to do something. Today's Saturday so they'll have you sitting at least for the weekend. For good reason, bail will probably be denied the first go-round. I'll have to resubmit the bail packet to the magistrate judge. She'll approve it. Chances are you're looking at two whole weeks. I'm just being honest."

"I expected as much. So what do they have?"

Diamond chuckled. "Come on. Aside from the assault, rather, spitting on the agent, the same shit they always have: nothing. What they did manage to do was get testimony from that piece of shit Douglass. This Agent Reddick sought a good faith warrant, meaning even though there wasn't any physical evidence to his claims and accusations, chances were more than likely they were true. It's all hearsay. The Feds are much different from the state. They actually convict off of strictly testimony, but your record is so spotless. Thanks to me, even with a court-appointed lawyer no jury will convict you. So due to double jeopardy standards, they would blow their chances of ever using a conviction on something that'll stick."

"What about everybody else they grabbed?"

"A few of them got minor weapons charges, for small shit like not renewing their gun permits. Nothing. Most of them are already out. You can't be charged. It's a public establishment. That stuff could've been anybody's. Besides, it wouldn't even make it to the evidence room."

"So this was their best shot?"

"Pretty much." Diamond lightly laughed as she agreed.

"Well, we haven't even swung yet. Let's get down to business. Here's what I need handled. Today, let's show 'em how hard we really go."

Diamond smiled and shook her head. "I figured you'd say that. I'm already on it."

Chapter Thirty-eight

Felicia stood behind Monica and watched her effortlessly put three holes in the targeted man's chest and three into his head. She professionally reclaimed her firm grip by placing her left hand under the butt of the gun along with the ball of her left foot planted in the ground balancing the weight as she slightly bent her knees and fully extended her arms, while squinting with her left eye closed. When she felt comfortable enough, she calmly exhaled then repeatedly pulled the trigger. The remaining five shots hit the man in his groin area leaving no trace of a crotch.

"Bitch, I'm impressed," Felicia announced and she thoroughly was.

Monica let out a light chuckle. She knew Felicia was studying her the entire time. She deliberately missed the main target a couple of times, careful not to draw suspicion about her accuracy. She lowered the Glock .40 and turned around. She removed her protective goggles. "It was a'ight," she said modestly.

She knew had it been a real person instead of a firing range target sheet, they wouldn't stand a chance. She had been handling guns for quite some time now and had studied some of the best marksmen around.

"Not bad." Felicia revealed how surprised she still was behind Monica's marksmanship. She had expected to see bullets whizzing all over the place and then, once Monica was done, she'd step in and show her how a pro did it. Despite Monica's pretty decent performance, that was still Felicia's plan. "Now it's my turn." A sinister grin appeared on her face.

Just as she put on the protective glasses and was about to take position, her phone went off. Unexpectedly, Monica's phone went off a second later. Felicia and Monica retrieved their iPhones at the same time. They both stared at their screens and then looked up at each other.

Chapter Thirty-nine

Careese was happy to stroll back into work. She entered with a smile plastered on her face the way she always did as if nothing had ever happened. She paid no attention to the dropped jaws and surprised looks on some of the faces she strolled by. Some of her coworkers looked as if they had seen a ghost. Her boss, Mr. Harry, was the only one who knew of her return. She made sure she looked awesome in her white two-piece Oscar de la Renta pantsuit. She went right to her post and relieved the temporary teller who had been filling in for her during her brief absence. She recounted her drawer and got set for a busy day. She hoped the time would go as slow as it wanted to. She needed time to settle back into the swing of things. She mustered up a welcoming look when she saw Olivia quickly making her way over to her.

"Are you all right?" was the first thing Olivia asked.

"Yes, I'm fine." Careese smiled.

"I missed you," Olivia whispered to Careese. She looked around before she brushed her hand gently across Careese's arm.

"Me too," Careese replied. Even without looking into her eyes, Careese knew that Olivia had fallen for her. Her reaction to her return only confirmed what she had already known. *Poor Livie,* Careese thought, knowing the feelings weren't mutual. She had used her coworker for what she had needed and she had served her purpose well.

"I'm glad you're back," Olivia chimed.

"Yeah, it was just a case of mistaken identity. I'm glad to be back too." Careese flashed a fake smile. Although she had no interest in her personally, she was still appreciative for the call Olivia had made on her behalf. Had she not, Careese knew things may have turned out totally differently. The two detectives had really worked her over and had her up against the ropes. There was no telling what would've happened had Diamond not shown up when she did.

"What do you say we do lunch?" Olivia asked, bringing Careese back to the present.

Careese shook the thought out of the forefront of her mind. "Sure," she agreed just to get rid of her so she could concentrate and forget about all that had happened.

Olivia smiled. "See you then." She scurried off as both of the lines began to grow.

It was business as usual and the day seemed to go as smooth as normal. Careese checked her watch. It was nearly time for lunch. She dreaded that she committed to lunch with Olivia. She did a quick scan of her line versus Olivia's. She hurried and withdrew money from her register to cash the check of the elderly lady who stood in front of her so she could service the other four people in line before her lunch break. She intended to place her LINE CLOSED/ NEXT WINDOW PLEASE sign up purposely to direct traffic Olivia's line so that their lunch date would be impossible.

"Would you like large bills?" Careese looked up at the elderly woman with a smile and asked. Her smile was immediately replaced with a frown as she became wide-eyed.

"Don't nobody fuckin' move!" were the words that echoed through the bank and sent customers and employees into a panic. The thunderous boom that rang out into the air was enough confirmation for everyone to let them know the robbers meant business. Careese froze. She could see one of the five masked men in expensive business suits subduing the security guard by the entrance of the bank by relieving him of his weapon. People screamed when they saw the robber butt the security guard in the head with the huge weapon, which sent him crashing to the floor.

"Shut the fuck up!" another one of the masked men bellowed as he let off another shot into the air. Screams turned into murmurs and silence.

Everyone instinctively dropped to the floor. In an instant, four of the gunmen were at the tellers, while the first one stood over the guard. Occasionally he peered out the window and glanced at his watch while he listened to a police scanner. "Six minutes!" he yelled to his partners.

"Fill 'em up!" one of the masked men yelled to a trembling Olivia as Careese and the other two tellers followed the same order. A large black duffel bag sat open at each of their feet.

One of the masked men made his way to where Harry, the bank manager, sat. "You." The gunman waved his weapon at Harry. "Get up!"

A wide-eyed Harry slowly rose. Apparently he had not complied quickly enough. The gunman yanked Harry up by the arm. "Give me a reason," the gunman threatened. He had his M16 pressed up against the back of the Harry's head. "Now move."

Careese studied Harry's face nervously. She hoped he didn't have anything stupid in mind.

Harry escorted the gunman to the back vault with his hands held high. A large light had switched from red to green.

"You got one chance to get it right or you die where you stand," the gunman warned.

The one thing Harry had in mind to foul up the robbery was immediately erased by the robber's threat. He wasted no time punching in the correct security code to the vault without triggering off the alarm.

The gunman smiled. "Good boy. Now, get in there and fill this bag up." He smacked Harry in the chest with the black duffle.

Harry entered the vault and began reaching for stacks of bills to stuff in the duffle.

"No, muthafucka, use the money on the left," the gunman ordered. "Down there." He pointed. "Small bills, none of those exploding dye packs and none of those black light specials that'll make my hand glow." The gunman was letting him know he was a professional. He stood over Harry and watched him close. "No! Those numbers are in sequence. Mix 'em up good! I know that trick, too!"

Once Harry was done, the gunman glanced at his watch. *Perfect timing,* he thought. Within minutes the duffle was filled to a T. "Thanks."

The gunman snatched the bag from Harry and then cracked him on the side of the face with his weapon. Harry was unconscious from the blunt force trauma to the head. He fell hard onto the some of the vault's money. The blood from his head flowed into some of the stacks. The gunman exited the vault just before it reclosed.

"Time!" the gunman up front yelled after hearing the radio dispatch letting all officers know there was a robbery in progress. The masked robber noticed his crime partners standing and waiting for him as he appeared from the back.

"Relax, folks, your money is safe. It's still in the back. I doubt y'all came to withdraw this much. So consider the rest ours. Thank you for your cooperation. You've all been lovely," the gunman slyly remarked before they attempted to make their getaway.

Careese finally let out a sigh of relief. She lay face down on the floor shaking her head in disbelief. *Just my luck,* she thought. She was glad that the robbery ended without any major incident. She couldn't wait to report the incident to her Double G sisters. Careese's thoughts were interrupted by the sudden presence of a figure. She hadn't heard anyone walk up, but she noticed the shadow that hovered over her.

Before she could turn around to see who stood over her, two rounds were pumped into the back of Careese's head followed by a note that landed on her back. The impact of the bullets caused her gold hair clamp to explode into pieces. Loud cries rang out as the gunman who had doubled back into the bank after forgetting why they had really chosen that particular branch to rob, quickly made his exit. He gave his crime partners the thumbs-up and then hopped on the Kawasaki that awaited him outside. Sirens could be heard wailing in the distance. The oldest of the Spaulding brothers popped a wheelie and pulled off, as his four brothers followed suit.

Chapter Forty

The unexpected knock at the door startled Loretta Douglass. Her eight-year-old daughter Cameron happily ran to the window hoping it was her father, who hadn't been home in two days. She was sad to see the two women in business suits on the doorstep. "It's for you, Mommy," little Cameron announced.

Loretta stood up embracing the last line of the news reporter's words about the bank robbery and cold-blooded murder before speeding up to the door. She was stressed out behind the fact that she didn't knowing whether her husband would ever make it home. They had spoken earlier and he had claimed to have worked out a major deal with the Feds. He also stated that he had given them a useful lead already, which looked good on his behalf. The test was just a waiting process. She hated that he had gotten himself in such a mess. She became angry all over again just thinking about it. Her train of thought was broken by the sound of the doorbell ringing for a second time.

"Just a minute," she yelled out as she made her way to the door. Loretta peered out of the small window and then opened the door. She cracked it as much as the chain would allow her to peek her head through the open space, while her daughter Cameron squeezed between her legs and did the same.

"Well aren't you just adorable," the first woman declared while bending down to meet her face to face before standing upright and introducing herself. Loretta studied the two women who appeared to have come from the black Impala with tints and a siren behind the front windshield. They were both in black pantsuits and had the usual navy blue wind-breakers with the large, high yellow FBI letters on the back.

"Yes, may I help you?" Loretta asked hesitantly.

"Yes, I'm Special Agent Marianne Peters and this is my partner, Violet Canan." The woman who introduced herself as Special Agent Marianne Peters smiled. She flashed held her gold badge up to the chained door. "We're from the Bureau."

"Oh, yes, please do come in." Loretta Douglass removed the chain from the door and opened it.

The two women stepped inside. "Thank you, ma'am. We've been sent here on behalf of your husband's sensitive case. We've come to interview y'all for the witness relocation process."

A sigh of relief swept through Loretta Douglass's body. "Okay, no problem, but how is he? Is he all right?" she wanted to know.

"Yes, he's fine. There's just some personal information that we need in order to properly provide a new identity for you and your family."

"Sure. Can I offer y'all anything to drink?" Loretta asked as Cameron sat on the sofa and started playing with her doll.

"Coffee would be lovely, straight, no sugar, thank you," Violet Canan stated.

"Same for me, thanks," Marianne Peters declared.

"Coming right up."

Within minutes, Loretta Douglass was back with two cups of joe.

"We're sorry to show up so unexpected, but we've been very busy. The funeral for our fellow agents is being held as we speak. It's actually live on television and then we got caught up with that bank robbery. Wasn't much we could've done there, so we felt that the safety of you and your daughter was more of a top priority. The outcome of the other two situations already played out. This is our prevention process right here. The women your husband is helping to take down are very powerful and will not be underestimated,"

"It's perfectly understandable. Thank you," Loretta expressed.

The three women all smiled at one another. "So, Mrs. Douglass, did you have any knowledge of your husband's criminal activities at all?"

Loretta Douglass took a deep breath. "None," she replied. "He hid it all from me well. Although, I did used to wonder where he would get certain things from, like his new car. He claimed it was a bonus from the department. He told me it was one of those seized vehicles from a drug sting that was up for auction. I found it kind of odd until his partner showed up with one too, making the same claims. So I let it go."

"Did he ever mention the organization that's causing all of this trouble? The Double Gs, as they call themselves?"

"Occasionally, like when something strange on the news popped up, he would associate it with them, speculating to himself. That's about it," she honestly recollected.

"And what did he tell you about the deal that's on the table for him now? The one that's going to bring y'all back together?"

"Just that he was being cooperative the best he could and we would be starting a new life far away."

"Did he go into details about the information he was providing?"

"None," she stated.

"You do know that what he is doing is very dangerous and very risky for the three of y'all. We have to tell you that it's no walk in the park. These women are professionals and very dangerous. Heartless if you ask me," Agent Peters proclaimed staring at her watch again.

"I'm learning as much, lately. Most of what I've heard was actually unbelievable. You just don't figure women to be so relentless," Loretta claimed. The interview was interrupted and Loretta Douglass's attention was drawn to the ringing house phone. "Will you excuse me?"

"Sure."

Loretta Douglass made her way over to the phone and picked it up. It was another collect call from her husband. "Oh, here he is now." She beamed. "He probably wants to know if you guys got here yet," she assumed as she listened to the recording. She pressed the number five on her touch tone as instructed. Her smile widened to its full extent.

"Hey, dear, I wasn't expecting to hear from you again," she announced. "No, everything's fine," she assured her husband, still smiling while fiddling with her thin chain. "Honey, I don't know why the guard would've told you it was an emergency and to call home. In fact, I couldn't be more safe. Two of the female agents are here interviewing me about your witness protection deal right now."

Her husband's reaction to her words startled Loretta Douglass. Before she could ask him what was wrong the cry of her daughter caused her to spin around. Loretta Douglass nearly fainted at the sight of the gun pointed against her daughter's head and the one pointed directly at her face. She immediately dropped the phone. "Please don't hurt my baby," Loretta Douglass begged. Tears spilled out of her eyes as her daughter Cameron stood there with her doll clenched to her chest with tearful eyes.

"Mommy," Cameron cried out. She tried to break free of the hold, but was yanked roughly by the woman who was introduced as Agent Canan.

"It's okay, honey," Loretta Douglass assured her daughter. "Everything's going to be okay."

The woman known as Agent Peters kneeled down and picked up the phone. The first thing she heard was Officer Douglass's cries. "Fuck you crying for now, pussy?" she mocked. "Isn't this is how you wanted it? For y'all to be somewhere together, far away in a beautiful place, with new identities." She let out an insane laugh. "I hear heaven's nice this time of year."

"No, please. I'll do anything, anything," Officer Douglass pleaded.

"Anything?" she asked.

"Yes! Anything." He put emphasis on his words.

"Okay, here's what I want you to do. I want you to suffer, suffer from knowing you caused this, and then I want you to wish you were dead with them and I want you to actually die, you cheese-eatin' rat motherfucka!" she spat. "Until then, what I want from your snitch ass is to never forget. Never forget this."

Douglass heard the phone being set on the counter. The next thing he heard were screams followed by two muffled shots, and loud thuds.

"Thank you for your cooperation, Officer Douglass," was the last thing he heard before the call was disconnected.

Chapter Forty-one

The televised funeral was intensely emotional. Speech after speech were being delivered by the loved ones and colleagues of each victim. Most of them were about the journey of each. It all deepened Agent McCarthy's guilt. He still felt responsible for each death. Even Agent Kelly's because he felt that he should've been there instead of Agent Reddick. It was his show, his operation. There was so much innocent blood on his hands. It stained. Never to be washed off. There was no going back in time. This would stick, forever. It would always affect his future decision making. Federal agents weren't supposed to feel. They were supposed to do. Do what it took. It was the exact same thing he instilled in his deep undercover agent posing as a Double G member. *What if she began to feel? Could she get the job done? Could she do what it takes? No.* It was the only truthful answer. So his mind was made up. It was time to pull her back out, before it was too late.

Right then and there, live, on national television, Agent McCarthy's convicting thoughts were interrupted and so was the entire funeral.

Agent McCarthy's daughter, Charlie's, eyes had rolled into the back of her head and she fell out of her seat, face first into the grass, and right in front of the three caskets.

Everyone gasped as they watched. Agent McCarthy and US Attorney Linda dropped to their knees, trying everything within their power to revive their only daughter whose pulse was dangerously faint and spaced far apart. Her eyes couldn't open and she definitely wasn't breathing. Agent Donahue tried CPR as Agent Constanza held her hands up screaming for medical assistance. They evaluated that an ambulance would never make it in time, but they were too scared to move her. The entire funeral came to a complete halt. Even the twenty-one soldiers rushed to the aid of the little girl. She was turning brighter shades of purple by the second and she still wasn't breathing. Agent Donahue continued to pinch her tiny nose and blow air into her lungs as Agent Constanza stood up from her knees and cleared the immediate space. Too many concerned people were closing in on them.

Agent McCarthy and his wife each held one of their baby girl's tiny hands while crying out. After a few more minutes, a helicopter hovered over the scene. Its propellers were strong. It blew away the empty plastic chairs and destroyed the tent over the podium and, even worse, the pictures and the flags that once sat on top of the caskets ripped away into the artificial wind. A medical team jumped out with a stretcher and loaded the McCarthys into the air lift.

"Imfuckingpossible!" Agent Reddick grunted while standing in the center of the crime scene, scratching his balding head out of pure frustration. He slowly removed his sunglasses and scanned the living room with no heartfelt compassion over anything other than losing a grip of his case.

At first, the federal detention center didn't take Officer Douglass's claims seriously. In fact, they had laughed at him as he approached the CO's station in a frantic panic. It took the most real tears he could pour out to show them his pain. They still took their time before they finally called up the chain of command. Eventually, the captain on duty checked with the ITS phone technicians and had the call replayed. He couldn't believe what he was actually hearing.

He immediately notified the local authorities and then the Federal Bureau.

After the locals had kicked in the door with their guns drawn, they quickly lowered them, surrendering, knowing they were too late. The killers were obviously long gone. But the angel of death was still there.

The bloody mess in the kitchen had been cleaned up. Loretta's body was placed back in the living room, sitting upright in the couch, next to her daughter. Both of her lifeless eyes were pulled back wide open to look as if they were watching the television in front of them. A single hole in the center of each of their foreheads was the only thing that didn't look calm and peaceful about them. An index card was planted in the arms of Cameron's doll. It read, WAR ISN'T ABOUT KILLING SOLDIERS, IT'S ABOUT PROTECTING THE CIVILIANS. NO ONE IS INNOCENT.

Agent Reddick slammed the card down hard on the coffee table and let it out a loud bellow. His cry nearly shook the walls.

Chapter Forty-two

Diamond parked her Range Rover in back of Club Panties. The front entrance had been boarded up and police tape was spread all around it. She made her way to and entered through the steel back door. She hit the switch to the only remaining light that wasn't busted out. When the room illuminated, an instant migraine appeared out of nowhere at the sight. It looked as if Hurricane Katrina had struck the area. She stepped over the debris as she slowly made her way upstairs to Starr's office. Reality smacked her hard in the face as she stepped in. The walls, floors, and couches had all been stripped. The aquarium glass tank had been shattered. Dead fish and the smell of them were inescapable. She got nauseated and quickly exited.

She headed back downstairs, all of the way to the sublevel. She walked through the dark tunnel and entered the Double G meeting room.

It was also torn apart. She went farther down to the private office. The round table in the Ovary Office was split in half, the shelves were stripped, and the file cabinets were empty and broken down. The expensive wall paintings that once hung were ripped apart. Tears of anger and sorrow filled Diamond's eyes at the sight. The entire club had been demolished and diminished, all except for one room.

Diamond entered the secret security room. The dozen monitors were still running. Many of the recorded CDs were removed, but she was sure the hard drive hadn't been erased. That would be giving the authorities more credit than they deserved, she knew. Just as she had figured, they hadn't thought that far. "Amateurs," she spat under her breath as she attempted to pull up everything that had happened, hoping to make sense of it all. She rewound back to when the FBI entered their establishment and started tearing things apart. After punching in an unlock code she had full access to whatever footage she wanted. She was grateful Starr had trusted her with the information.

She started with the hidden cameras in Starr's office. She gritted her teeth at the image that appeared on the screen. A sense of jealousy and betrayal swept through her body. She knew it would only anger her if she sat and watched, but she made a mental note of it. Now was not the time for her to allow her personal feelings to take precedence over the bigger picture. She fast-forwarded past the sexual episode with Starr, Felicia, and Monica. She stopped when she saw the familiar image of someone.

"What the hell?" Diamond's spider senses immediately went off. Despite being a member, she knew the person had no business being there by herself. Diamond watched as the culprit cautiously snooped around like a police dog.

"What the fuck is she looking for?" she asked no one in particular. Coming up empty-handed, she watched as the girl exited the office. Diamond continued to sit, rewind, fast-forward and watch for the next hour. Aside from one of her sisters being out of place and out of pocket, she was still coming up with nothing. She was sure she was missing something. *Think, D,* she told herself. She was certain she was overlooking something.

She squinted her eyes as she carefully studied the footage. Out of nowhere, a thought came to mind. Diamond rewound to the part of the recording she had decided to bypass. She jealously watched the sexual escapade in its entirety. She had already told herself she'd deal with that matter at a later date. Right now, she had to stay focused for not only Starr, but for herself and the rest of the organization. There was no way she was going to sleep or could sleep for that matter, while her boss/lover was locked down. There was no doubt in her mind that Starr could handle any situation she was put in, but she could not stand to see someone she loved confined. They had talked about worst-case scenarios in the past and what Diamond should do in the event one came to light. That day had come. Starr was incarcerated and Diamond knew what she had to do, needed to do.

She lightly chuckled at the cat fight between Starr and Agent Constanza as she continued to search for the smallest of clues in the video surveillance. She watched as the agents spilled out of the room one by one with Starr in tow. That's when she noticed what she had missed the first time around. It was quick, but not quick enough for her not to notice it the second time around. She watched closely as Monica scooped up the cell phone that Starr had dropped with her pants. Her eyes grew cold. "Fucking bitch!" Diamond cursed.

She leaned in closer to the screen to her left and turned up the audio. The one to her right had ended and appeared snowy on the screen. She was hoping to hear something to go off it but audio was inaudible. She stuck a blank CD in the hard drive's slot and recorded the entire scene she had just witnessed. She smiled to herself for a job well done. "Gotcha!" she stated matter-of-factly aloud.

Just as she was about to remove the disc, she noticed out of her peripheral vision that the screen to her right had now come back on. An image appeared on the it. Diamond drew her attention to the screen. Her eyes nearly jumped out of their sockets behind what she saw.

"What the fuck is this bitch doing?" she questioned as she squinted her eyes.

This time it wasn't Monica she was referring to. Confused would be an understatement to describe Diamond's feelings right now. It wasn't until she saw the Double G member remove something from under the Ovary Office's desk that it all became clear to her.

Diamond stuck another disc in the recorder.

"You sneaky-ass motherfucka," Diamond blurted out as she waited for the footage to download.

Minutes later she ejected the new disc and tucked it, along with the first disc, into her purse. She shut everything off, then stood and made her way to the service elevator. Her mind was all over the place. She was hurt and angry by what she had witnessed Starr partaking in, but she was more angry behind the new piece of information she had just come across.

Nobody crosses the Double Gs and gets away with it, was her final thought as she exited the elevator and strutted her way out of Club Panties. She knew the information she possessed in her purse was priceless. The value of it was enough for her to decide not to reveal it to Starr or anybody else for that matter. At least until she figured out the perfect time to do so. With Starr now behind bars, she knew she had to be the eyes and ears of the organization. After seeing what she had just witnessed on the monitor's screen, she decided it was time for her to step up to the plate and temporarily take charge of the Double Gs.

To Be Continued